FIVE SELVES

FIVE SELVES

Emanuela Barasch-Rubinstein

www.hhousebooks.com

Hardback ISBN   978-1-909374-91-1

Paperback ISBN   978-1-909374-79-9

Epub   978-1-909374-80-5

Front Cover: Mother & Child by Moshe Tamir 1954. Reproduced by kind permission of Presler Private Museum, Tel Aviv, Israel.

Cover design by Ken Dawson
http://www.ccovers.co.uk/

Typeset by handebooks.co.uk

Published in the USA and UK

Holland House Books
Holland House
47 Greenham Road
Newbury, Berkshire RG14 7HY
United Kingdom

Holland House

www.hhousebooks.com

In memory of my mother, passionate and observant,

Bertha Barasch

Acknowledgments

I began writing this book after the death of my father, Moshe Barasch. His loss created a need to express the pain through art. The process of writing made me further appreciate the spirit both he and my mother, Bertha Barasch, had given me.

I am deeply indebted to Aharon Appelfeld, for his wise words and fierce support. Without him I would have never ventured to publish the book. I am extremely fortunate to have Robert Peett as an editor and publisher; one could not hope for any better. My thanks to Miriam Gross (Lady Owen) for her support, praise, and valuable suggestions. Jill Claster Midonick, a scholar and a dear friend, offered encouragement and assistance, for which I am truly grateful. I would also like to thank David De Meza for his insights and friendship. Yigal Presler of the Presler Private Museum generously gave me permission to put Moshe Tamir's picture on the cover. Hai Tzabar of Magnes Press offered help and good advice.

Last but not least, the loving support and belief of my family, Yona, Alon, Eran and Yuval, is what made writing possible.

FIVE SELVES

A Bird Flight

A couple of hours after the death of my father I received an invitation to a conference in Chicago. We took what was left in the locker - some books, blankets, slippers, his watch - and we were about to leave the eighth floor of the hospital with its blinding lights, never to return. We were waiting for the formal arrangements to be completed, and stood forsaken, first in the corridor, then in the elevator, and finally on the ground floor of the hospital, which was somewhat dark and gloomy. At this late night hour the entrance hall was almost empty, and we sat there useless, expecting nothing.

When the documents were ready we drove away, attempting to grasp the death that had taken hold of us. As we arrived at my parents' home, I got a message inviting me to give a lecture in Chicago, at a conference titled 'Life and Death - Representations in Art'. I ignored the message, which normally would have evoked much excitement. We sat silently: my mother's words that 'he lived a long and good life' emphasized the unintelligibility of this absence. We didn't dare enter his study, full of books which seemed so orphaned now.

Many spoke at his funeral, among them a famous writer whose wise words began to make the presence of death more familiar. The announcement of his death at the entrance to the house surprised me. The big, black letters proved that he had died more than his fresh grave did. The crowd of people who came to the house, the concluding ceremony of the *Shiva*, the Psalms verses we read at the cemetery—all these made me forget the invitation to the conference. But as the mourning week ended, I recalled the possibility of a journey. At first I thought I would cancel my participation, but then I changed my mind— the dark house, his paintings on the walls, my photographs in his study, they all made me wish I was somewhere else. I sent a message that in spite of the death of my father I would be attending the conference.

The organizer of the conference, a young professor of Italian descent, replied immediately. He expressed his condolences politely, didn't forget to add some personal notes to the old clichés, and offered to pick me up at the airport upon my arrival in Chicago. Though I knew him from his visits in Haifa, I felt that meeting him at the airport, something more usual with close friends and family members, would be embarrassing and even irksome. Also, his intentions were unclear. Was this the offer of a young host acting in a punctilious, protective manner, or maybe an implied, more personal suggestion that we would meet again during the conference? When I saw him during his visits in Haifa I always felt there was something unclear about him. He almost never expressed himself unequivocally; between the words there was always an ironic tone, somewhat derisive. There was also something deceptive about his appearance. Though he was a handsome man, always dressed in an elegant and reserved manner, his face bright and clear, as he spoke his upper lip would extend forward, seemingly a deliberate attempt to appear refined, as if he found it hard to talk but he was making an effort for the sake of others. Straight hair, perfect teeth, bright eyes, though somehow turbid, his appearance lacked a flaw that would make its advantages stand out.

When I told my family I intended to participate in the conference they were somewhat surprised. Indeed, my mother kept saying that one has to return to daily routine as soon as possible, and my sister expressed a similar view. However, I felt that they were suppressing a profound condemnation, one that had nothing to do with my journey and therefore should not be articulated in one breath with the mourning customs. My youngest daughter, unlike them, was franker and expressed some resentment. With her typical childish candor, especially when her own desires were at stake, she said she wished I would be present at the *Chanukah* party in which she had a special part, and added immediately, breathlessly, that it is inappropriate that I travel so soon after my father's death. The way she entwines her childish needs with moral arguments always makes me smile. She hugged me softly, her rosy, rounded cheek close to my face, confessed she would miss me immensely, and retired to her room.

My oldest daughter, with the sparkling eyes, said nothing, but her look suggested contemplation untypical of her age. She watched me as if my journey concealed a secret she wanted to expose. Like most young people she was almost constantly immersed in daily experience; it seemed as if she was reliving certain moments over and over again. But once in a while, not very often, there was a different, almost oppressive, curiosity in her look. Despite my obvious resentment she kept asking me about the purpose of my journey. My explanations of professional interests, the importance of conferences, the need to meet with colleagues, did not satisfy her. She inquired about the weather, about whether I would be staying close to the lake she'd heard of, about the time difference between Chicago and Haifa, and more questions on the travel itself. Finally she got tired and closed her eyes. Her face looked weary. I promised to call her, but the promise was worthless; not because she was afraid I would break it, she was absolutely sure it would be kept, but since she felt it further concealed the secret of my voyage. And so, late at night, we fell asleep one next to the other, in the light of the tiny lamp in her bedroom.

Strangely, Eviatar was indifferent to my traveling. At night, as I told him about my plans, he pretended to be surprised but it was clear that his distracted mind was inattentive to my wanderlust. In a tired voice he began asking about various practical details—the girls' daily routine, food, home arrangements, the cat: it seemed that all these were added to the endless concerns bothering him. His straight hair fell on the pillow and his black, rounded eyelashes, looking as if they were made by an artist, fluttered a bit before they covered his blue eyes. Just before he fell asleep he said something about 'an interesting subject', though I never told him what the conference was about nor the title of my lecture. He turned his back to me, pulled the blanket, and I was left bare and shivering, trying to get back the pleasant warmth of the bedclothes.

And so, a week later, I was standing at the airport with Eviatar and the girls, presenting my passport to a heavily made-up attendant, checking in my suitcase and saying goodbye to my family. In my handbag I had the script of my lecture, which I was hoping to read once again during the flight, some books, a photograph of my father that I decided at the last moment to take with me, and some stationery. After I entered the airplane and found my seat, an older woman sat down next to me, and at once began staring at photographs she took from her bag, and crying. Eagerly she told me that she had left her son in Carmiel and was returning to Argentina, where her daughter awaited her. Her grief made me forget the circumstances of my travel. I found myself absorbed in the figures in the photos: her forty-year-old son, with long, black hair, his wife smiling excessively at the camera; their two young boys; and the older woman in the company of her son and his family, staring amiably at the unknown spectator.

The plane took off and I relaxed in my seat, ready for the long way. Since I traveled by myself I was hoping to take advantage of the flight to examine my lecture. But as the flight progressed I became distracted. I placed the script of the lecture on my knees, after a couple of words I couldn't concentrate anymore. The images of my father's last days surfaced, and their effect was even stronger now. It seemed that every detail existed separately, and was not part of a sequence of events that preceded and followed it. Also, the memories from the last weeks of his life seemed obscure, and in particular I was reminded of a certain event, against my will. During a visit to my parents' place I entered the bedroom to talk to my father, who had lain down to rest. But he fell asleep and was steeped in a dream, apparently experiencing great happiness. He muttered some unclear words, yet it wasn't the words but the overwhelming childish expression of joy that struck me. I stood there motionless, staring at him, immersed in his gaiety, and then I left the room. Now, as during my visit, I knew the source of his happiness would remain unknown, but still I had the feeling that it was a childhood experience that overtook him. From the old face peeked a young boy, cuddling his mother or challenging her. And though I kept trying to ignore the enigma of his dream it emerged again and again, forcing me to try to solve it.

The Argentinian woman sitting next to me also relaxed in her seat. It seemed as if the distress of the separation from the beloved son had somewhat dissipated and now she was preparing for an encounter at the end of her journey. She spoke again of her son, but after a few sentences she began telling me about her daughter, her face revealing the expectation of her return home. The young grandchildren, the toys scattered about her home, the apartment on a high floor over a main avenue, the small car she had left for her daughter and now surely needed some maintenance work—in her spirit she was already there, in the familiar place, so distant from the displaced son in Carmiel. And though she kept looking at the photo of her son and his family she seemed unfocused, and then put the photos back in her wallet.

After a couple of hours I felt sleepy. The lights in the airplane were dim, most passengers took a nap, and so did I. I sank into a deep, dreamless sleep. When I woke up the airplane was fully lit, ready for breakfast before landing. Many passengers were walking restlessly to and fro. I got up and walked to the galley, feeling that I couldn't take the discomfort of the voyage anymore. And indeed, after a light meal, the trays were collected and the plane began to descend, heading towards Chicago.

As soon as we landed everyone hurried to the passport control. Grave-looking officers awaited us, and after a while I approached the counter. As I took my passport out of my purse to hand it to the officer I saw that the photograph of my father had been left in it. In this photo he was still a young man, with a rounded face and dark, heavy-framed glasses, his face full of light that was in his eyes, not in his smile. Quickly I removed the photo from the passport, and since I had to respond rapidly to the officer's requests, I tossed it into my handbag. I passed through passport control, picked up my black suitcase and, rolling it along, walked with hesitant steps towards the exit.

In spite of my decided efforts not to look for the young professor, I couldn't help my wandering gaze, watching the people who waited at the exit. Focused on the passengers coming out, they looked at no one in particular: Men in elegant suits, women carrying children, drivers holding papers with names, staring expectantly, and then with disappointment, at every approaching passenger.

I was relieved as I was certain he was not waiting for me. Already during the flight I had imagined how awkward it would be to meet him. Now I was happy that I could avoid it. I walked briskly towards the taxi station when someone grabbed my arm.

As I turned around I saw again the ridiculing smile, the straight teeth, the bright eyes. He shook my hand, said how happy he was that I had come in spite of being in mourning; he again expressed his condolences, and offered to carry my suitcase. His light, straight hair was a bit out of place; apparently the wild winds outside created some disorder in his tidy haircut. Though he was trying to be sympathetic, he glanced aside in a distracted manner. His fastidious questions about my flight, as if he was envisaging the entire way from Haifa to Chicago, revealed a strange curiosity regarding trivial, unimportant details: What food was served on the way? Why was the flight half an hour late? Did I have to wait a long time before I passed through passport control? While he was engaged in this peculiar interest in my travel, we walked to his car in the parking lot. He put my luggage in the trunk and we began driving towards the city.

We drove fast along a wide highway, surrounded by neon lights and immense colorful billboards. Though I am not used to driving on highways, this one seemed to direct its drivers quickly to their destination; cars joining the road from various directions, everyone rushing simultaneously to the same place, hastening to overtake each other. After about half an hour the skyscrapers of Chicago began to rise in the distance. The twilight glaze illuminated the city in mauve, and an abundance of miniature lights gradually materialized into the outlines of luminous skyscrapers and tall buildings, inviting any stranger to assimilate into their endless lights without questioning him about his life circumstances.

On the way my young host was more focused, keeping his mind on the driving. He told me a bit about the city and its various quarters, explaining that he lives on the north side but that my hotel is in the center of downtown. He seemed surprised when I showed some disappointment that we weren't passing by the lake; he explained that we were arriving from the west side while the lake is in the east, and promising that tomorrow we would drive along its shore. The certainty that we would meet again outside the conference spoiled the moments of pure joy that come from an unfamiliar place. My mind was distracted from the fast drive, which now transformed into a slow ride through narrow streets at the center of the town. Against my wish I couldn't help wondering, again, what his intentions were. The dark streets beneath tall buildings passed before my eyes almost unobserved.

When we arrived at the hotel he hastened to take out the suitcase, hand it to the concierge, hurriedly shake my hand, and drive away. In my room I tried to read my lecture but exhaustion overtook me. I managed to call home to say that I had arrived safely. My youngest daughter answered the phone, and in her childish way told me about her day in detail. Finally we said goodbye and I fell asleep.

When I arrived at the conference hall the next morning, I immediately noticed him. My young host, the organizer of the conference, was dressed in an elegant suit. No doubt he saw me as I came in, but I got the impression that he was trying to avoid me.

After some small talk and an introductory speech, the participants began to discuss their work. I also read my paper, but although I tried to present it in an appealing manner, a new, unfamiliar fatigue overtook me. The arguments that previously seemed fascinating now sounded dull. Throughout the presentation I couldn't help wondering whether my words were coherent. The sentences seemed detached from each other, the grammar bizarre, unusual. And also, my very presence at the conference suddenly seemed so unnecessary, even embarrassing and unclear. During the lecture I suddenly recalled the Rabbi from my father's funeral. His exact, detailed orders regarding the mourning customs had surprised me, but now they were fully comprehensible and justified. My thoughts traveled to the cemetery, and as a result I made several mistakes reading the lecture. Finally, as I concluded, some people in the audience insisted they had questions, so I had to return to the lecture room, whose bare walls were now full of florescent light, and pretend that my arguments made some sense. When the lecture was done everyone thanked me; I was disappointed that the usual relief when concluding a presentation was immediately transformed into deep exhaustion. But as I was about to leave the conference , the young professor appeared, smiling cordially, revealing his straight teeth, with, in his eye, as always, a spark of scorn.

He invited me to join him for lunch with some of his colleagues. Since I couldn't think of a convincing excuse I drifted along with the others. The odors in the large dining room, its wide windows with their view of the Chicago River, the hustle and laughter in the room—they all eased my exhaustion, and I engaged in conversation with people I had never met. However, I was determined to leave immediately after lunch and take a nap at the hotel.

Once the dishes and food residues disappeared from the tables, everyone got up and walked to the lecture rooms. I decided to take advantage of this moment; I slipped to the stairway, went one floor down, and turned quickly to the revolving door. As I stepped out the cold wind hit me. I felt that my coat, which wasn't suitable for this climate, didn't provide any shelter from the cold air. Still, I advanced to the street, directly towards the river. It was a cloudy day; the soft, vague light was comforting. I found myself standing between two bridges, behind one of which was the lake. I stood staring at the flowing water, not sure whether I should go directly to the hotel or take a short walk on the lakeshore. The tall buildings were reflected in the water, slightly trembling, adopting round shapes and then straightening again. I looked up. The skyscrapers' heads disappeared in a thick screen of clouds, and it made them look heavy and graceless. I felt a light touch on my shoulder. Behind me stood the young host, smiling, as if concealing a secret.

He began to talk without pause. He is also very tired, the conference is indeed interesting but too full, he can't focus on so many lectures. And apart from that he is very busy lately; he began to spell out all the issues he has to deal with these days, and how he was not sleeping well at night, probably due to the whistling of wild winds. I felt that his flow of speech was taking him over, and he was wondering how to stop it. Finally, almost in a whisper, he suggested he would take me for a ride alongside the lake. I was embarrassed to recall that yesterday I had expressed a desire to see it. And so, after a couple of minutes, we were in his car on a road following the curves of the lakeshore.

The clouds that filled the sky were mirrored in the lake, and the dark gray water was stormy. I never saw such a color, the Mediterranean never captures the tone of the sky in such a way. And most surprising was the heavy fog, so dense that the horizon disappeared; you couldn't tell where the water ended and the sky began. Next to this immense gray screen the city looked small, in spite of its tall buildings.

At first, my host was absorbed in descriptions of the landscape, adding humorous anecdotes about the city's past days: Frightening Mafia men, strange mayors, revolutionary unions—he made them all part of a long story, a chain of tales through Chicago's wild past. But in spite of the many details, after a couple of minutes the funny stories ended, and now he tried to direct the conversation to me. He asked about people he knew in Haifa, told me about his long acquaintance with some of them, and even revealed some little-known facts regarding their past.

As this conversation concluded he seemed embarrassed, and began to ask me how I had been feeling since the death of my father. Though it was obvious that he found the subject oppressive, he kept talking about it. Casually he mentioned that his mother had died two months earlier, at a relatively young age, but added nothing on the circumstances of her death. I hesitated, unsure whether I should ask. But I felt I didn't have enough strength to say even a couple of simple, polite words on someone else's mourning, so I decided to remain silent. For a moment I thought he wouldn't talk any more about my father's death, but immediately I apprehended, by his strained face, that he had no intention of changing the subject, and perhaps this was the very reason for his invitation to drive along the lake.

My host seemed very alert now; the touch of scorn in his eyes had completely disappeared. His handsome face revealed profound tension, which couldn't be concealed. After half an hour's drive he turned to one of the small inlets on the shore, drove to the parking lot, and stopped the car facing the skyscrapers on the lakeshore. The sight was breathtaking. For a moment I completely forgot my uneasy host and was absorbed in the picture composed of endless shades of whites and grays, the straight lines of the buildings contrasting with the soft, round clouds surrounding them. He cleared his throat, trying to break the awkward silence. Then, unexpectedly, as if we shared a secret, he asked what exactly my father had died of.

I murmured something about a combination of diseases, each one treatable in itself, a weakness of the body, offered a word about childhood maladies that had deformed his lungs. I was hoping to sink once again into the view of the city, now surrounded by dark heavy clouds; it seemed as if it was about to disappear. But my host insisted, and I realized he was waiting for a detailed answer. I turned and looked at him. His clear features and ridiculing eyes were full of discomfort, a light blush spread through his face, blurring the clean lines.

I tried to remember the exact medical details, but they seemed remote and incomprehensible. I recalled a visit of a senior doctor at the hospital, but I couldn't remember anything he said. Maybe something about 'atmospheric pressure', perhaps 'support', I think the word 'potassium' came up— only my father's tormented face emerged, his thin, fragile body wrapped in engraved skin. But my host kept burdening me with questions. He seemed fascinated by the most trivial medical details, inquiring about the causes of my father's disease, the reasons for his hospitalization, when he lost consciousness, attempting to reconstruct some profound truth hidden beyond the specific details of the process of dying.

I tried to say something about the beauty of the city but saw it was in vain. My host insisted, and it was clear he had no intention of halting his inquiry until he could collect all the facts. The embarrassment was gone; he was completely engrossed in the medical description. To his disappointment I couldn't reconstruct the details, even though it all had happened only a couple of days ago. The brightly lit hospital sank and disappeared, and all the facts that had seemed so vital just two days earlier were now beyond my comprehension. I was ashamed to admit that I couldn't remember the names of the doctors, and I never knew the medical terms. But the more hesitant my answers, the more determined he was to extract the facts that seemed to him so simple, so ridiculously easy to remember. And when I couldn't recall the name of a certain medication the mocking look appeared once again, though he tried to conceal it.

To my relief fierce lightning and thunder alarmed us, and rain began to fall. It stopped the flow of questions and made me more at ease. It was impossible to ignore his disappointed countenance. Embarrassment had evaporated, and he was no longer concealing his desire to clarify in his mind—even somehow appropriate—the process of my father's death. I was expecting an explanation, perhaps a hesitant apology, but he acted like someone whose secret had been revealed, and his shame was now replaced, with a loud sigh, by relief. Not only did he not apologize, but his eyes betrayed resentment that the rain interrupted his questions.

I suggested we leave the parking lot, and he began driving southward, towards downtown. The heavy rain slowed the traffic, and I could examine the approaching buildings. Though it was still early afternoon, darkness covered the city. Heavy, opaque clouds created an impression it was night time, the high waves made the lake on our left side look wild and alive, its tone dark gray, more like the familiar sea at Haifa. We drove in silence. The people on the street were running to find shelter. A surge of lightning lit the sky. The cars going south towards the city drove at a very low speed, some turning into side streets to avoid the congestion. Once again the roofs of the buildings disappeared within the clouds, and this incomplete image, like a picture whose upper part had been ripped, made me feel distressed. The buildings looked so heavy, as if they were pressed onto the street, threatening to create a huge hole in the ground and to destroy it.

After about half an hour we returned to the place where the conference was being held. I found it hard to meet his eyes, but I asked my host if he could drive me to the hotel since I was tired and wished to get some rest. He agreed politely, again with a spark of ridicule, entirely indifferent to the exposure of his excessive interest in my father's death. His features became clean and handsome, lacking the distortion of human perversion.

When he dropped me at the entrance of the hotel I felt so exhausted that I couldn't even say goodbye politely; I got out of the car, went into the hotel, and withdrew immediately to my room.

I sank into the bed. The heavy curtains were drawn and even the dimmest light didn't penetrate. Only a small lamp was turned on in the corner of the room; the walls were decorated with dark and somewhat depressing pictures. The shadows cast by the furniture seemed as alive as the objects themselves, and in this gloom the golden bedside cupboard stood out strangely.

My eyes were heavy and almost closed, but I couldn't fall asleep. The disturbing questions of my host surfaced, but they remained unanswered, distressing and perplexing. His entire interest in my father's death was suddenly natural, and made perfect sense. In vain I tried to recall the names of the medications. The medical information was completely nebulous but I could clearly see my father's body, lying on the bed as a ventilator was inserting life into him and sucking it out. Unconscious, surrounded by endless tubes, he seemed like a complete stranger, and it was impossible to recognize the man that he was. His vital, sharp expression was replaced by a deep coma, and my attempts to trace the familiar features were futile. It seemed to me that a terrible mistake was taking place here, and we were all gathered around the bed of another old man, a stranger, to witness his death. By his body you could tell he had reached a very old age—apparently he ate very little in his last years since he was skinny, and the tone of his face was grayish, almost silver, creating the notion that he was already in the process of passing to another world. Wrapped in a hospital robe, tubes and needles piercing his thin body, the dreary light of the hospital didn't bother him at all, and he was entirely indifferent to the loud whistles of the machine inserting oxygen into his lungs.

A loud ring broke the silence in the room. Quickly I deserted the sights of the hospital and hurried, with relief, to the telephone. I was so glad to hear my oldest daughter, she with the glaring eyes. She had a long list of questions: what does the city look like, how big is the lake, what is the weather, did I have a chance to tour the city, where was I staying, and more and more. I tried to insert some short sentences in between her questions but failed. Finally, when she was exhausted, I told her a little about the tall buildings, the silver lake, the gloomy hotel, and some details about my lecture. Once her curiosity was satisfied she wanted to hang up but I clung to the young voice, which even from a distance was fresh, eager to escape memories of the hospital. I inquired how they were handling the daily routine without me and found out she was alone at home, and about to go to a friend. My youngest daughter hadn't come home yet; Eviatar would be back late at night. When I ran out of questions I had no choice but to say goodbye; however I made her promise to call me again the next day. I sank again onto the bed, relaxing between the blankets. The warmth that spread through the room made me drowsy. And so I woke up the next morning with the first rays of sun penetrating through the thin gap between the curtains.

In spite of my desire to tour Chicago, I decided to attend the second day of the conference. Fear of distressing memories led me to choose the lectures, though the sights of the city seen from the taxi on the way to the lecture hall made me even more eager to wander in the streets. It was a clear, cold morning, the clouds that covered the sky yesterday had disappeared, and a soft, pleasant sunlight fondled the buildings. The skyscrapers stood tall, a puzzle of forms and colors. They passed before my eyes quickly, I couldn't grasp many details; I felt as if every building was concealing a secret that could be revealed only by looking at it slowly and patiently; the observer had both to immerse himself in the details and to ignore them. But in a couple of minutes the taxi arrived at the conference hall, and after a brief look at the Chicago River, now entirely blue, I entered the lecture hall.

I was a bit late, and the lecture had already begun. The silver-haired speaker, looking very dignified, began to present his study. The room was crowded, and everyone seemed fully focused on his presentation about Medieval descriptions of death. But after a couple of minutes his arguments became tedious, and the audience seemed somewhat weary. People began looking around, examining who was present. I also explored the room curiously. To my right sat a woman about my age, looking elegant and distinguished, with a perfect hairdo, her countenance revealing that she wasn't finding the lecture interesting but was nonetheless determined to listen to it until the very last word. To my left sat a redheaded man, clearly bored. As I looked around my eyes met the gaze of the young host.

In his elegant clothes he seemed stiffer than usual, and this emphasized even further his excessive refinement. When he saw me he nodded seriously. I stared at the lecturer, immersed in an elaborate description of life in the Middle Ages and felt my gaze becoming vague. In spite of the white light on the podium his figure seemed unclear, the sharp lines of the table were blurring. To my great relief the lecture came to an end; everyone clapped, and left the hall for a break.

I hurried outside with the redheaded man to have coffee. In vain I waited to feel the light touch of my host. Despite of my full confidence that he would approach me now, and my ready answers regarding my busy schedule today, he disappeared. Casually I turned to look around, to see where he was standing, but among the strange faces I couldn't find the familiar eyes and the protruding lip. And so I drifted with the crowd to another lecture, and afterwards we all went to lunch.

The redheaded man, am Irish professor, amused me with stories about his lodgings on a very small island with very few inhabitants. The stories about the isolated island, the bright dining room, the Chicago River seen from the large window, and the soft winter sun made me feel better. I was almost at ease, and felt that I could even enjoy the conference a little. Together with the others I got up from the table, squeaking the chair back to its place, and turned again to the lecture hall. And when this presentation was over I went outside, determined to walk to the hotel.

The biting cold surprised me. A deceiving winter sun created an expectation of a moderate temperature, but I realized the air was colder than yesterday. In the bright light the contours of the city were sharper, inviting the observer to see an abundance of forms; it was difficult to focus on one without diverting your gaze to another just as fascinating. I began to walk towards the nearest bridge in order to cross the river, careful not to touch the people passing by me in spite of looking upwards, towards the buildings. More than anything I was surprised by the mixture of new buildings, half-transparent, with the older houses of the city, also carefully designed in soft, pastel colors, decorated with many ledges and knobs. Yet as I was walking a feeling of constant incompetence overtook me: already then I knew that when I tried to recall the sights of the city I wouldn't be able to fully reconstruct them.

I walked along the main avenue, hoping to see the city in its full splendor. The river was calmer now, the water less opaque. I stepped onto the bridge, which was trembling from the many cars driving on it, and turned on to Michigan Avenue. People paced rapidly in the wide sidewalks, elegantly dressed, entering luxurious stores with expressions of moderate gravity, and leaving it with shy, childish smiles. Businessmen in suits, expensively dressed and tailored women, groups of teenage girls, a couple of black kids who drummed beautifully on upside-down pots to the applause of passers-by, and a sad saxophone playing in the distance, a tune so strange to the bustling city. I walked along the avenue, attempting to absorb my impressions of the foreign place, giving in to a pleasure I could never resist: the first sight of a street I had never seen before.

As I reached the end of the avenue I was surprised to see the lake again, now light blue, calm, like an empty hammock swinging lightly in the wind. I turned around, and in order to see more of the city I decided to walk back along a street parallel to Michigan Avenue. Older, heavier houses stood there, a big church, hurried couriers carrying parcels—I began to feel tired and wished to return to the hotel to take a rest. I crossed the river again, now on a bridge made of bare steel, heavier, lacking the grace of Michigan Avenue, but perhaps more true to the spirit of the city. I reached the Loop as I paced under railroad tracks hung in the air, and was surprised by the squeal of a stopping train. I walked among people wrapped in dark heavy winter coats until I reached the hotel.

I was on my way to my room when the receptionist handed me an envelope left for me. I grabbed it and went up to the room, sinking onto the bed in the dim light. In this twilight time the room was almost completely dark. As I tried to draw the curtains I realized that the window faced a high wall; the curtains were not intended to obscure the light infiltrating into the room but to prevent its inhabitants from looking outside. Next to the bed stood a small, over-embellished lamp. I turned it on, and under its yellow light I opened the envelope to find a note that my young host had left for me. In small, rounded handwriting he thanked me for yesterday's tour along the lake—though it was abruptly interrupted by the heavy rain—and asked if we could meet tonight; he would call later and was hoping I wouldn't be too tired.

My exhaustion was so deep that it blurred my resentment about the note. I wanted to rest at the hotel for a while and then wander through the streets, to do some shopping. Now I realized that I would have to spend the evening in the company of the host. Maybe I could choose to reject the invitation, or even say nothing at all—the short walk had made me so tired that the wavering between accepting and rejecting the invitation was postponed, and I fell into deep, comfortable sleep.

When I woke up I tried to guess how long I had slept. The heavy curtains left the room dark all through the day. I looked for the electric clock, but it was blinking endlessly, indicating that at five o'clock it had been disconnected from the electric power. The warm coziness under the blanket kept me in bed. I tried to recall the walk in the city. The abundance of details disappeared, and only a few sights were left: a square entrance to an old building, a store selling bizarre objects for perfect comfort, a unique skyscraper made of stone and glass, a saleswoman with a heavy southern accent wearing a dark pink shirt; and nothing more. In spite of my efforts to remember more details of the walk, all that came, against my will, were the sights of the hospital. It seemed that even the smell of the hospital spread in the hotel room. I recalled the long hours besides the aching body of my father, as it made strange whistles due to the artificial ventilator. Exhausted from the sight of the strange man we sat in the waiting hall, and it seemed that the other people sitting there were also expecting nothing, but, like us, couldn't leave.

Suddenly the head nurse came, calling us to follow her. Fearful of bitter news I entered the room last, but then, to my surprise, my sister said 'Daddy woke up'. We all stood around the bed, looking alertly at the closed eyes, listening to the hiss of the machine. First the eyelids moved, a shiver of intense effort, and then, slowly, the eyes opened. Immediately the lifeless, feeble old man disappeared from the bed and in his place my father appeared, his expression as lively and penetrating as ever, even with a glimpse of joy at seeing us. Without saying a word there was no doubt he understood very well what had happened.

He seemed surprised to see us, but when we told him that he couldn't speak because of a tube piercing his throat and asked him if he understood us, he moved his eyelids to inform us that he was indeed present here, speaking our language.

The doors of the hospital room opened widely and bright daylight penetrated, warming the patients in their beds, wrapped with identical robes, embracing the sunrays so rare in this building.

The sound of the telephone ringing transferred me at once to the hotel room in Chicago. The receptionist announced that someone was calling me, and before I could come to my senses and detach myself from the distant hospital, I heard the voice of my young host. He asked how I was feeling, wished to know if I had enjoyed the lectures today, and wondered if I had managed to see at least part of the beautiful city. He spoke so quietly that I could hardly hear him. Almost in a whisper he asked if we could meet tonight, and invited me for dinner. He added, in a casual manner, that this time he promised to be more amusing than in our previous encounter, and offered to take me to his favorite Italian restaurant.

I think the conversation was over before I said a single word. My host spoke as if I accepted his invitation without me uttering anything. In spite of his quiet speech he wasn't waiting for a response, but was involved in his plans, the odors of the Italian cooking were filling his senses and he couldn't imagine that I didn't want to spend my last evening in Chicago with him. I tried to recall when he said he would pick me up, but couldn't determine whether it was seven or eight o'clock. I sat on the bed, staring at the phone, wondering if there was any escape, yet realizing there was no way to avoid the dinner that had been forced upon me. For a moment I thought I could call and say I was not feeling well, but I couldn't help thinking it would be futile. I was left lying on the bed, motionless, staring at the lamp with the yellow light, waiting for a sign that my young host had come to pick me.

Apparently I fell asleep again, since a telephone ring woke me from a dreamless slumber, and even though I heard the voice of my host I couldn't join the syllables into words. In the background I heard cars blowing their horns and the squeaky voice of the receptionist, so I gathered he was waiting in the lobby. I wanted to apologize, to say that I would be there as soon as possible, but again the call ended without my saying a single word. Suddenly there was silence; it seemed it was agreed that I would come downstairs. I stayed in the room for a little while longer, ignoring the endless ringing of the phone, and finally I descended to the lobby. My host sat in his car, waiting for me, alert, forced to ignore car horns protesting about his lingering in a prohibited place too long.

Quickly I entered the car, and even before he said hello he was driving. After some polite words he began describing in detail the restaurant that we would be dining in tonight. He knew it well: not only did he know the entire menu by heart but he also added a couple of words on each dish, like an expert witness weighing the pros and cons, attempting to emphasize the advantages and not what is lacking. We drove in crowded streets and turned again to Michigan Avenue; in addition to its permanent lights, miniature Christmas light bulbs decorated the trees. The strong wind in the avenue jolted the trees fiercely, and the abundance of lights looked like a strong stream that would engulf the people in the avenue.

As I managed to avert my eyes for a moment from the glittering, I realized that my young host had concluded his survey of the various dishes and now he was telling me about the Italian family that runs the restaurant. Gracefully and with a touch of humor he described the father of the family: a huge man dominating his employees, entirely devoted to the preservation of authentic Italian recipes. And indeed, as we entered the restaurant he greeted us loudly, and finally we sat at the table and ordered food.

My concern that he would inquire about my father proved false. Again he looked as if speaking required a special effort, his upper lip protruded forward; his bright, straight hair fell forward gracefully as he was engrossed in the meal. Even though I could see he was expecting this dinner, he spoke about the food in an arrogant manner, as if he had happened to walk into the restaurant by chance. He told me about certain events that took place at the conference, spiced them with funny tales about the lecturers, and in a whisper shared embarrassing facts about some of them. After a couple of drinks his exaggerated refinement turned into haughtiness. He didn't take the trouble to conceal his scornful gaze. As I put out my hand to hold a glass of wine he grabbed it, in the pretense of a narrator attempting to emphasize part of his story, and didn't let go until I was forced to giggle. The wine made me sad and I had to double my efforts to chuckle from his stories.

As I was thinking how to hint that I was tired and needed to return to the hotel without spoiling his joyous mood, he surprised me and confessed he was exhausted and wished to go to sleep early tonight. He paid, exchanged a couple of pleasantries with the owner of the restaurant, and we went outside to the parked car. He insisted on opening the car door for me, and only then did he sit in the driver's seat. I couldn't help observing that he was a bit drunk, and I was worried how he would drive to the hotel. He managed to exit the parking lot and with an evident effort merged with the traffic on the highway. Again we drove southwards towards downtown, sometimes getting too close to other cars, often hearing blowing horns. But my host seemed very cheerful and now he began telling me something about a woman he used to date. There was no logical sequence in his words; the different events he was talking about made it impossible to determine which happened before the other.

I was relieved that heavy traffic made him slow down and adjust to the monotonous speed of the stream of southbound cars. Though he tried to overtake some of them, after a couple of minutes he had no choice but to accept his place in a line that was advancing at a moderate and constant pace towards the towers of Chicago, which at this night hour were so full of lights, much more than a wandering look could contain.

After a couple of minutes in which he insisted on telling an inexplicable story, he suddenly realized he was driving the wrong way. Instead of turning directly to the hotel he kept driving along the lake, prolonging the journey: the lakeshore led us directly to a bridge hanging over the Chicago River, and there was the city, resplendent. I felt as if I was looking at a postcard of a distant city, but Lake Shore Drive was leading us directly into the postcard, granting us a rare opportunity to view endless beams reflected in the river, and the huge black lake next to it.

After a couple of minutes we got to the hotel. He found it hard to say goodbye; instead he grabbed my arm as he continued the inexplicable story about that woman; his eyes couldn't contain the overwhelming contempt any more. It seemed as if he was looking for a way to conclude the story, which he too found obscure. As I realized there was no escape, I pulled my arm away abruptly and rudely got out of the car, annoyed by the story of this strange, unknown woman. He didn't look surprised by my sudden departure. On the contrary, looking at me with a hint of laughter, he waved and drove away.

I went to my room and lay on the bed, staring at the yellow wall and wondering why I had accepted the invitation to spend my last evening in Chicago with the host, who, when I was leaving him, didn't look so young; his intoxication emptied his face of its clean and smooth appearance and made him look somewhat silly. The yellow light in the room was depressing. I managed to get up and turn it off, and then sank into the wide bed again, staring at the lamp with old leaf-like silver decorations. Somehow a pleasant light spread now in the room, probably coming from a streetlamp close to the window. Through the heavy curtains concealing the nearby building the light filtered into the room, creating a bluish luster. Suddenly the voices of a man and woman could be heard, first dissonant and then transforming into cries. The woman's voice was maudlin; the man's tone indicated that he was trying to assist her. But she kept sighing, as if she was in pain. I thought perhaps she is in labor, since her voice became loud and aching. The man also began crying, but it was unclear whether it was a result of anger or despair.

The painful noises took me back to the hospital. As my father gained consciousness he seemed to recuperate slightly. After a couple of days he was detached from the whistling machine, and then we could even have some conversations. First, he asked what had happened to him. We couldn't avoid revealing the severity of his condition, but he asked several times how was he 'returned' here. Yet in the coming days he began to groan repeatedly, and once again his thin body was pierced with tubes. He dozed for hours, as though the return to the gloomy room was exhausting, and perhaps even undesirable.

At noon, as I was standing beside his bed, there were suddenly sounds of clattering and tinkling. Everyone looked around and saw that the room was shaking a bit, even the heavy beds were trembling. A minor earthquake taking place near the Dead Sea shook the room on the eighth floor of the hospital. Cries of fear and excitement came from everywhere. Amused I looked at the tubes, suddenly full of life, but as I turned my gaze to my father, I saw he was suffocating.

At first my cries couldn't be heard above the loud shouting in the room, but finally doctors rushed to his bed and began treating his ill body. They ordered me to leave, and so I did, even though he asked me explicitly to remain by his bedside. I waited outside, and soon family members joined me. We sat there for long hours watching the closed door, attempting to glance at his bed, which now was concealed by a heavy curtain. Every time the door opened we asked to see him, but beyond the curtain only coughing and murmuring were heard. Finally the curtain was drawn slightly and I went into the room. He was lying on the bed, shivering, his feet left bare. As I asked him why he was not fully covered he said he didn't know and pointed to a brown blanket on a chair. I placed it on his feet. Then again I was asked to leave.

A couple of hours later a doctor came out of the room; his solemn face left no room for doubt. He began a long explanation about my father's twisted heart and stiff lungs, and after the medical information stated that he must be reconnected to the hissing machine, since he was unable to breathe independently. He listened quietly to our questions on the nature of the medical procedure, and then looked at us with soft, brown eyes. Adopting a professional tone he said he believed my father wouldn't survive the night. Then he suggested that we see him before the tubes are inserted again into his body.

When we entered the room the doctors had told him that he would be put to sleep and reconnected to the machine. Broken words and promises were all we could offer, but he, unlike us, was focused on the medical details. Years of illness had taught him to examine numbers and to assess the gravity of his condition, and now he was attempting to make an accurate evaluation. As his breath became heavier we were asked to leave the room. We were left in the corridor, listening to the dim voices behind the closed door. My mother, illuminated by the white light of the corridor, refused to take part in our silence. I wished she would, but as she said that my father 'is very tensed now' I realized how well she knew him.

After a further couple of hours the doctor returned. Again we demanded to know how he was, and together with him we entered the room. On the huge bed lay an old man, his entire body punctured with tubes, making all sorts of squeaks; he seemed to be in a deep coma. His skin was almost transparent, blood vessels were visible beneath the thin and fragile cover, his eyes were closed, and only the whistle of the machine was heard in the room; at that late hour the lights were finally dimmed. We stared at him, searching for a spark of life, but then the doctor's voice was heard, saying that he must be disconnected from the hissing machine because he was dead.

The doctor suggested that we leave the room for a couple of minutes, and then we would be able to 'part' from him.

And so, after hesitations and with some resentment, I entered the room to see him once more. Strangely, now that his body was void of tubes and the machine was silenced, he resembled himself again. I recalled a photo of him at a young age that I once saw, thin and extremely solemn, his eyes shut and his countenance betraying profound melancholic contemplation.

Embarrassed at demonstrating emotions confronting the dead, the kiss I gave him on his forehead seemed tasteless and bitter; in fact I considered staying out of the room, but the fear of the moment passing was overwhelming, and so I put my lips on the round, transparent forehead and left the room quickly.

The first rays of sunlight penetrated the hotel room. Steeped in the sights of the hospital, I fell asleep on the high bed. I recalled the voices from the next room, but there was silence now. The soft beams filtering through the curtains made the room look faintly orange, and somewhat warmer than yesterday, in the yellowish light of the golden lamp. I remembered the tedious evening in the company of my young host, the depressing dinner, his drunken smile, the story of the strange woman, and now I was glad that I wouldn't have to see him again. Slowly I got up from the bed, and switched off the lamp; out of habit I drew the curtains to look outside. I forgot that from this window only the bare concrete wall of the next building could be seen. I closed the curtains and turned on the lamp with the yellowish light; against the background of dawn its light seemed more orange. I removed the suitcase from the closet and tossed in my clothes, some papers I had brought with me, and stationery. The suitcase, which had been almost empty at my arrival, was now full and round. I could hardly fasten its zipper and place it on its wheels.

Eager to escape from the orange room, I rolled the suitcase to the hallway. I closed the door behind me and it shut in silence. Though my flight was scheduled to leave in a couple of hours, I felt I couldn't take the curtains concealing the concrete wall any more. I went down to the reception, paid for my stay, and got out of the hotel.

Cold air hit my face. Bright daylight filled the street, the light of a winter sun, its rays heralding sharp, penetrating freezing cold rather than pleasant warmth. I walked with the rounded suitcase into the street, waiting for the taxi that would drive me to the airport. The air was unusually pellucid, the colors of the buildings clearer, and now unpleasant corners could be seen— some mold under a window, a broken gutter, a light brown wall that had turned grayish. The passers-by were fully covered, attempting to defend their cheeks from the wind's bite.

After a couple of minutes the taxi arrived. The driver tossed my luggage into the trunk and we were on our way to the airport. First we drove in narrow streets, crowded with people and cars even at this early hour. Above us passed the train, again making a harsh, loud cry, stopping in haste, as if it was surprised to find a station. Everyone was in a hurry, perhaps rushing to get to work on time or maybe trying to escape the hazardously translucent air outside. The taxi kept moving, crossing less elegant streets where bare steel could be seen in walls and in small bridges. The stylish houses disappeared, and now I saw small lodgings, brownish gray, their windows covered with curtains. After a few minutes' drive the taxi got onto the highway, which was heavily congested in spite of its immense width.

The speedy drive comforted me. As the driver accelerated I was relieved; nothing soothes a grieving soul like the sights of the passing road. Residential houses, illuminated billboards, huge trucks racing forwards, and above all, a constant movement, which even though it fails to provide a bird's-eye view brings humanity closer to flight than anything else. Objects appear and disappear quickly; everything on the way would pass in a flash.

The taxi slowed at an intersection, but as the driver turned to the left lane he hastened forward, blowing his horn at a car that had gone astray. After a couple of minutes the signs indicated that we were close to the airport. I looked upward and saw many airplanes, some looking as if they weren't moving at all, others descending, cruising slowly above the city, waiting patiently for their turn to land in Chicago.

In a short time we arrived at the airport. Again I felt the biting cold. After the driver quickly unloaded my luggage, I grabbed the rounded suitcase and hurried into the terminal, looking for the airline's counters. The lights in the terminal seemed too bright, since the morning rays filtered inside without revealing their freezing transparency. I began walking along the counters as I felt a gentle, almost unnoticeable, touch on my shoulder. Apparently I had bumped into another passenger's bags. I turned my head. My young host stood there in front of me.

Wrapped in a heavy coat, scarf, and gloves, he tried to conceal his profound embarrassment, but it was evident. His eyes lacked their usual ridiculing expression; red spots covered his face, betraying a discontent that he would have to admit that we hadn't met here by accident, and there was no escape from acknowledging that he had gotten up early in the morning and driven to the airport only to meet me. His straight hair was somehow colorless, his soft hands looked strained though he wasn't carrying any luggage. After a moment of hesitation I asked him why he had come to the airport. I felt that if I pretended that he was waiting for a flight I would only make his embarrassment more blatant.

He suggested that we have coffee. We made our way to a somewhat dark coffee shop, crowded at this early morning hour, and after a couple of moments we found a vacant table. He went to get the coffee.

At the next table a group of young Korean girls were immersed in lively conversation, speaking passionately. Elegantly dressed and well made up, their lean bodies moved abruptly to the rhythm of their voices. As I was listening to the click of their tongues my host came, holding two steaming cups of coffee. He murmured something about not taking sugar in his drink, attempting to postpone the moment in which he would have to explain his presence at the airport.

I smiled politely. A weariness took me and prevented me from making even the smallest gesture, which would have made the confession, not yet articulated, easier. I wanted to fall asleep; I sipped the coffee, hoping it would awaken my curiosity, which seemed to have evaporated. After a few seconds of silence he said in an aloof tone that his mother had died several weeks earlier. Staring at his cup he told me, in an indifferent voice, that she had been ill for a couple of months, and had deteriorated rapidly. He elaborated on the nature of the disease, how it took root in her body and then distorted it. Clearly he was an expert in the medical terminology and had learned it thoroughly; for a moment it seemed he took pleasure in articulating the long names of the medications his mother had been taking. The anatomical description of the dying mother lasted several minutes, answering questions, never asked, about the birth of the disease, its development, and triumph.

I was so tired I feared my head would drop on the table. The Korean girls got up in a bustle, making way for an old dreary couple, sipping their coffee silently and eating with a manifested engagement in the process of consumption. Since the coffee shop was a windowless room, the bright morning light was blocked; it was lit by tiny light bulbs. My young host kept staring at the cup, moving it slowly between his hands.

He was completely absorbed by the depiction of the disease. Even though I tried to follow it, I couldn't understand what exactly had caused her death. I was attempting to comprehend at least in what parts of her body the disease had struck, but in vain. The stream of medical terms increased constantly. It was clear that my host didn't see that I couldn't understand what he was saying. His head inclined forward, his straight hair falling on his face, the red spots that covered his face having disappeared, his eyes now lacking any contempt—he seemed eager to reach a most complete and accurate description of her sickness and death.

Realizing there was no hope of understanding him, I was utterly overtaken by my fatigue. I was afraid my eyes would close and that I would doze off. Again I drank coffee to overcome it, but it was futile. The dullness of the coffee shop and the elaborate medical explanation made me sleepy. For an instant my young host diverted his gaze from the table to me, and realized then that I was finding it hard to follow the description. He dropped the medical details and began to describe a profound dispute between two experts regarding the nature of the disease and what was needed to defeat it. As he explained the point of view of each doctor one could have imagined that his mother is still alive; the depiction was so vivid it created an impression that if only he would choose the correct way of treating the disease the sick mother would be saved.

Soon the long sentences got shorter and it seemed that my young host was hesitating about how to phrase the medical conclusions. Profound weakness prevented me from offering condolences. I was trying to murmur a cliché on how death is part of life, but all I could do was adopt a sympathetic countenance, perhaps even nod once in a while.

Finally silence fell. Again red patches emerged on his skin, and his eyes, now completely void of contempt, were staring at the dark space of the coffee shop. At last he began to move impatiently, reclining in a way that suggested he was about to get up. He held the two cups before removing them from the table, and in a slightly hoarse voice said that he thought he had mistakenly adopted the advice of one of the experts, and that had he followed the advice of the other one his mother would still be alive.

I couldn't help looking into his eyes: his gaze was wandering, unfocused, surveying the coffee shop without observing anyone. For a moment I thought I finally saw the defect so lacking in his appearance. But he got up quickly, turned around, and without saying anything stepped towards the exit, taking the cups in order to put them somewhere. His straight hair, the heavy coat, the hands shaking though they carried nothing, were all gone; I was left alone in the coffee shop. I saw that the old couple that sat at the next table had left, and now an elegant old man was sitting there reading the paper, oblivious to my staring at him.

Immediately after my host left I tried to understand the description of the disease, but now it seemed even more pointless. In spite of my attempts I was unable to imagine the sick mother wearing a robe, lying in a white bed. The complicated descriptions of the disease removed the depressing smell of the hospital, the neon lights in the corridors, the matter-of-fact expression of the staff; the fear of the inescapable and the innate desire to succumb and accept death as it comes.

Apparently I sat there for a long time, staring at the people who changed frequently, because suddenly I heard an announcement that passengers on the flight to Tel Aviv were boarding now. Quickly I picked up my luggage and hurried to find the gate. After a couple of minutes I was sitting comfortably in my seat on the plane, covered with a blanket, attempting to fall into a deep, dreamless sleep. Soon the aircraft took off and turned east, but I couldn't sleep, and against my will the image of my father rose in my mind.

In his last year he was extremely weak. When we came to visit he had to rest in his room, though he wanted to spend time with us. One evening, as we were about to leave, I entered his room. He lay in his bed, his eyes closed, the radio quietly broadcasting a news report, and there was no knowing if he was listening or if his spirit was elsewhere. His hearing had declined so he didn't notice I was in the room; I stood there, watching him in his bed, in complete solitude, perhaps present, perhaps not. His hands, which I loved watching when I was a child, masculine hands with a perfect balance between the paintbrush they once held firmly and the intellectual occupation he practiced throughout most of his life, were now heavy and large, with dark, protruding blood veins, holding the black radio. In the dim light of the half-dark room, illuminated by a five-branched chandelier with only one bulb on now, he looked like an old man lying on a rock, covered with a heavy blanket, his grey hair wild. Finally I approached him and spoke in a loud voice; he opened his eyes, smiled at me gladly, and said that he had listened to the news broadcast and he was sorry I was leaving. I kissed him on his forehead and went.

Suddenly turbulence made the aircraft move abruptly. Cries were heard from the front seats, a baby was weeping, awoken from his sleep by the lurching move. The flight attendants hurried to pass along the aisles, ensuring that the seat belts were fastened. I noticed that a handsome man with a short beard, about fifty years old and somewhat elegantly dressed, was sitting next to me, completely immersed in reading. Apparently he was not satisfied with the book, for every now and then he made a gesture of discontent, and once he even giggled out loud. Impolitely he ignored the flight attendants, who approached him several times, reading the book and steeped in his aversion to its content.

The sharp movement made him divert his attention from the book, which had a scent of fresh paper. His big, blue eyes explored the plane with a gaze that might have appeared condescending, seeming distant and uninvolved. First he looked out the window, from which an infinite space and a dazzling light could be seen; then he looked forward, following the baby's cry, which was heard throughout the airplane; finally he turned and looked at me, examining me with manifest indifference. My eyes met his; his face remained still. He appeared completely self-absorbed. I wanted to say something about the fear of the plane swinging in a cloudless sky, but his expression suggested disgust at the idle conversation we might have.

As the rocking decreased he returned to his book, still reading it with distaste. I tried to peek at the book but it was impossible. Boredom made me examine him again; for some obscure reason his blazer attracted my attention, its fabric having a delicate pattern in brown shades. I was thinking how impolite it was of me to stare at him like that, but he was so engrossed in the book that he didn't notice.

I looked elsewhere. I decided to examine the lady sitting on my other side. But she turned away from me, fully covered herself and fell asleep, and all I could see was gray hair, dull and curly, on one side of the blanket, and bare crossed feet on the other side. Her worn-out shoes were dropped under the seat, while the thin legs and bony feet hung in the air—it was hard to imagine what she looked like. The covered body seemed very slim and fragile; I was thinking that it would be impossible to tell her age. And so, again, I turned to look at the reading passenger. I couldn't help examining his blazer very carefully.

The symmetrical design, the delicate shades of brown, seemed so familiar. Nothing is as irritating as an attempt to trace a latent memory. I was wondering where I could have seen it, where the fabric was manufactured, whether this fabric could also be used for ladies' clothes. But in vain. The delicate material remained familiar, yet my attempts to uncover its secret were fruitless. My efforts exhausted me. After a couple of minutes I decided to stop, and closed my eyes. Dim voices came to me: the softly weeping baby, a lively conversation between two women, the repeated questions of the flight attendant about whether the passengers would like a drink, all heard against the background of a constant stream of air and the light sweeping sound of the plane.

Apparently I slept a little. As I woke up the lost memory emerged; my father had a blazer made of the same fabric as that of the man sitting next to me. Many years earlier, when I was about six or seven years old, he would put it on when he was flying to Europe, usually during the summer. On the morning of his departure he would be elegantly dressed, smelling pleasantly, freshly shaved, engrossed in his traveling plans but anxious about the moment of parting from his children. As the taxi came I couldn't hide my tears, and then he disappeared. Months later he descended from the stairs of an airplane, wearing the same blazer, but now it was somewhat sloppy, his shirt hanging down from his pants, and he was carrying heavy suitcases.

Now that the puzzle of the blazer was solved, another disturbing memory surfaced and wouldn't go away. Once, as my father returned from abroad, he opened the suitcases on the rug and took out the presents he had bought us. First he drew out a big, beautiful doll and happily gave it to me. It was evident that the doll, large, black-eyed and blond, was good-natured and cheerful; the light smile on her rounded, red cheeks revealed a lively character, even mischievous. And my joy doubled when I found that if she was turned upside down the sound 'mommy' came out of her mouth. But my father kept giving out the presents he had brought to other family members, and gradually I realized that the only thing that I was going to get was the graceful doll, whereas others got many presents. My mother sensed my disappointment, said something to my father in a low voice, and even asked him in German if this was my only present. He admitted it was, with sorrow and agitation. I stopped myself from crying until I was in bed. My mother came to my bed and whispered that although I got only one doll it was very pricey. I told her she was right and that I wasn't angry, waiting impatiently for her to leave the room, so I could give in to disappointment and pain.

The dim anger awakened by this memory was distressing. In spite of the mourning I couldn't forget the old disappointment, which became more real and concrete the more I thought about its details. The doll had not only a mischievous face that made me love her instantly but also a strong body, very different from most dolls, which tend to be rounded. My father brought so many presents to the others that they couldn't hold them all together, and they were cluttered on the rug; his expression as he apologized in German, revealed that absent-mindedness had created this error, and now he was deeply sorry; my mother was rebuking him, careful not to raise her voice.

The childish sorrow awakened was ridiculous, even shameful. I tried to think of the hospital, the cold, bright light, the huge beds in which skinny people lay, their bodies pierced with needles, but it all seemed so distant that I couldn't even envisage the distressing sight of the room in which my father had died. But the painful memory of the doll prevailed, against my will, animated and alive.

In order to escape the old anger I looked at the passenger next to me. Again he we reading, but I noticed that now it was another book; his face revealed profound pleasure. He was so absorbed that I felt I could examine him uninterruptedly. Fully concentrated, his blue eyes followed the lines rapidly. The short beard created a dignified, spiritual look, perhaps even puritanical; he wore a white shirt, not very clean, with the collar tucked under the blazer—the sight was now even more distressing than before.

Suddenly I felt a deep hunger, like bird's claws stuck in my stomach, an insatiable hunger that seemed like it could never be satisfied. I was relieved as the smell of a warm meal began spreading through the airplane. The food carts approached my seat, stopping to serve passengers hesitating which dish they would eat. Finally the food tray was placed before me, steaming with a strong odor of meat. Though the wrapping was scalding I removed it in haste, tore the cover of the utensils, and bit into the boiling food. I could feel my tongue and lips burning, but the claws tearing my stomach made me eat the hot beef. I concluded my meal in a flash but was left hungry, as if I had eaten nothing.

I looked at my neighbor for the journey; he ate slowly, concentrated on the taste of the food in the same way he read the book. His light skin turned pinkish, and in his eyes was a glimpse of haughtiness.

When the flight attendant returned I had to overcome my shame and ask for more food. I ate the buns she brought immediately, almost unconsciously. When she passed in the aisle again I apologized humbly, murmuring something about not having eaten since yesterday, and she brought some more buns, which were eaten in haste, almost whole. I asked for drinks, which were served over and over again. Only after many long minutes did I sit comfortably in my seat, wondering if the hunger was fully satisfied.

I placed my head on the headrest and felt it was made of soft, gentle fabric, unlike the coarse one covering the seat. The touch was so pleasant, I swung my head constantly to feel its fondling. My head leaned backwards, I closed my eyes and tried not to think of the hunger that hadn't fully subsided. I covered myself with the light wool blanket and tried to sleep, but then came a strong smell of feminine fragrance. Apparently one of the passengers had put on some perfume, perhaps in order to eliminate the smell of the food. The scent was intoxicating: a combination of chrysanthemum, orange blossom, freshly cut grass, and perhaps a hint of lemon. I inhaled the blossom spreading in the airplane, driving away for a short while the mechanical stream of air accompanied by constant whistles. There is nothing like the true pleasure of lovely fragrance, as if one has been transported in a flash to fields with wild flowers and blooming fruit trees. Sometime exotic spices are mixed in— but perfume can never contain the smell of the sea. I inhaled the scent time and again, wishing to preserve it, but slowly it evaporated.

A pleasant glow spread through the airplane. A few passengers closed the small window shade; the light wasn't dazzling anymore, but gentle and soft, with a white undertone. It seemed like a ray piercing the clouds, though the plane was cruising in a cloudless sky. In this tender light the passengers looked relaxed, dozing or talking in low, pleasant voices. The man next to me began reading again. Apparently it was the book he liked, since he seemed to take pleasure in it.

I also sat comfortably, succumbing to the delicate radiance, and fell asleep. I was awakened by the voice of the flight attendant announcing that we were approaching our destination, and should prepare for landing. Immediately I grabbed my purse, searching for my passport. In between its pages I found again the old photo of my father. I held it, feeling its wave-like ends, and my fingers touched his face.

My father's smile radiated from the old paper, vital and full of light. He had big eyeglasses, with black frames and rounded lenses. The glasses seemed heavy and bulky, but nothing in his countenance supported such an impression. On the contrary, from beneath the lenses covering his eyebrows emerged illuminated eyes, focusing on the photographer yet pretending to notice him only by accident. His skin, which over the years became almost transparent, still carried the signs of youth. Though it was a black-and-white photo, he seemed a bit rosy, or perhaps it was the soft luster surrounding him in the picture. Clearly he was attempting to look serious, but a light smile glowed on his face, though it was impossible to tell how exactly it was revealed. He had had this smile for a long time, but in his last years, when the distress of old age couldn't be ignored anymore, it disappeared, and in its place came a spark of despair, which he tried to conceal. From behind his glasses, now entirely transparent, emerged a new gaze, unfamiliar, of someone who knows the end is near and that any attempt to preserve the moment is doomed.

Unintentionally I caressed the photo with my fingers. The soft cheeks, the dark, wavy hair, the heavy glasses, the old summer suit, they were all blended with a tear that dropped on the photo, absorbed into the old paper, leaving a new stain on my father's suit. Attempting to stop the tears I looked aside. I saw that the plane was about to land, and the landscape of Tel Aviv was already visible from the windows. The sky was clear, without the smallest cloud, and only one bird could be seen from a distance, perhaps black, perhaps blue, escorting the plane that was about to hit the ground with a huge thump and bring its passengers to their destination.

Earrings

Grandma squinted to see better. She examined the earrings in the box meticulously, turning each one from side to side to see it from a different angle. Several times she picked up one of them and placed it against the light, and then returned it to its place in the black tray. After a couple of minutes she turned to me and asked if I would like to have a pair of earrings. I wanted the stud ones, with tiny, iridescent sapphire stones set in gentle gold fittings, their color strong; but since they were so small they looked more like two-dimensional painted decorations than like heavy pieces of jewelry. Grandma held them carefully, examining them, and finally she said they were lovely and she would be glad to purchase them for me.

The earrings were placed in a small box, wrapped with crackling cellophane paper. Grandma paid, and we stepped out to the street. Immediately she began praising my choice, saying that she also would have chosen these earrings, and added that they complement my light, straight hair and my eyes. She loved jewelry. In addition to her wedding ring she had two rather large rings, each one with a different gemstone, one green, the other bluish purple. Circling her neck whenever she went out was a pearl necklace. Her clothes were elegant: straight-lined dresses stitched by an expert dressmaker and made of fine fabric. Her gray hair was perfectly coiffed, tied behind the head in a way that emphasized its gentle soft tone, with a golden hairpin. In black shoes with high heels she walked on the pavement, erect and graceful; she looked like those European women one sees in old films, pacing calmly in wide avenues, watching the passersby with a distant gaze.

And indeed, Grandma was born in Vienna after the First World War. A daughter of a wealthy family of fabric traders, she was sent to a boarding school for well-born girls, where mostly she acquired good manners. But she loathed the other girls, their forced smiles and outbursts of anger, and after endless pleadings her parents consented to take her back home. She was enrolled in a school in the city and immersed herself completely in her studies.

When the Nazis seized power, her parents decided to move to London. The luxurious house was rented out and the family moved to an elegant villa, surrounded by a wide garden. During the war Grandma was a nurse in a hospital treating wounded soldiers. She met Max there, a Jewish soldier who had joined His Majesty's Infantry. Max was wounded in both legs, but the loving hands of the pretty nurse helped him overcome pain and begin walking. They paced slowly in the hospital garden, he telling her about his life before the war and she supporting him, making sure that he would walk slowly, according to the doctor's orders.

After a couple of months they got married. But the war mutilated Max's heart; the walking skeletons he had seen haunted him in his sleep; worst of all were their wide-open eyes, staring at him as if he was a weird, distorted figure that must be watched. A couple of months after their marriage Max suggested that he and his young wife leave their home in London and settle in Palestine. Grandma agreed instantly, and the couple moved to Tel Aviv.

Their pretty home in a neighborhood full of trees made the young couple peaceful. Max completed his engineering studies and Grandma began working at the Jewish Agency as a translator of German documents. After three years my mother, Esther, was born, and two years later they had their younger daughter.

Grandma tried to educate her daughters in the same way she was brought up, but in spite of her immense efforts the daughters rejected the European spirit and began acting like their classmates. She was surprised to see that they shouted at their friends even though they weren't quarrelling, and she also recognized that they were attached to their friends in ways unfamiliar to her. Esther had a redheaded, freckled friend, a tall, intelligent girl, and the two girls used to speak on the phone for hours. Grandma tried to inquire what they talked about for so long. Esther answered that she was telling her friend anything that bothered her and the friend was telling her everything that happened to her.

Grandma could remember her childhood friends in Vienna, quiet, reserved girls, wearing school uniforms, chuckling as they spoke of teachers and whispering about older brothers of their schoolmates. It never occurred to her that she could tell her friend everything that was happening to her. After school she used to walk home with Isabella, but only rarely did they meet in the afternoon. On the way home they reconstructed the day's events, complained about homework, and sometimes laughed about fat or silly girls. But when they separated and Grandma went home, the presence of Isabella evaporated and materialized again only the next morning.

Grandma used to think that her daughter's friendship with the redheaded girl would become oppressive, a burden, like a personal shortcoming. Though she never knew why she felt this way, she tried to distance her daughter from her friend, but in vain. The girls spent many hours together, giggling or immersed in intense conversations which stopped abruptly every time Grandma passed by the room. She once heard Esther tell her friend that her mom didn't want them to be friends. Grandma was alarmed, but to her surprise the sentence evoked bursts of laughter and some whispering she couldn't understand.

Much to Grandma's dismay, her two daughters often mocked their parents' European upbringing, and they often said that it was preventing Grandma from fully integrating in Israel. Every time she waited patiently in a queue, someone would take advantage of her good manners and get ahead of her. In the loud disputes that erupted once in a while she would have to give up, since she couldn't scream like the others. The girls saw her limitations and didn't know whether they felt sorry for her, or angry that she couldn't defend them and take proper care of their needs.

But her greatest surprise was the teacher-parent conferences at the daughters' elementary school. Esther's teacher flipped through her grades, said she was doing well but didn't study enough, and then went into a long appreciation of her social skills. The teacher said that all the children in the class want to be her friends; Esther was very 'dominant', yet didn't force her wishes and choices on others. Grandma was so taken by surprise that she forgot to ask about her achievements in math, a subject she knew Esther found difficult. She felt that all those compliments were concealing something, but didn't know exactly what it was. A year later the very same conversation took place but with another teacher, and similar conversations with her younger daughter's teachers. After that Grandma stopped asking about their intellectual achievements and settled for the report card they brought twice a year.

As the years passed the rift between Grandma and her daughters became wider and deeper. Esther had several boyfriends, but the relationships always ended in despair, a deep pain she shared only with her friends. Grandma's advice in these matters seemed to her drawn from an ancient long-dead world. Even when she quarreled with the redheaded childhood friend and looked devastated, she refused to talk about it with her mom. Grandma realized she couldn't comfort her daughter anymore; the opportunity to support her was long gone, and now there was no way to reproach her for mistakes of the past.

Esther met my father, Yaron, at the university. Wearing ragged jeans and an oversized shirt she sat on the grass with friends, and he joined the company and sat by her. During their conversation he drew a dry leaf from her untamed hair and threw it away gracefully. Esther followed the leaf gliding in the air, and as she shifted her gaze she saw the tall student watching her with deep concentration. Yaron smiled, told her that he had invited some friends to his room that evening and he would be glad if she joined them.

As she approached the building, she heard loud laughter coming out of the windows on the second floor along with the scent of cheap food. She hesitated for a moment then decided to enter. Yaron's friends welcomed her with smiles and jokes, and in a couple of minutes she felt at ease, like a person who has been absent from home due to a long journey and upon whose return suddenly everything seems strange; but she knows that this sensation will soon be replaced by a perfect homey coziness.

Their wedding took place in the backyard of Yaron's parents' home. In spite of her joy, Grandma couldn't help feeling somewhat sour; this was not how she had imagined her daughter's marriage. The Rabbi made tasteless jokes, the guests were dressed in a way she thought was becoming for a school party and not a wedding, loud giggling was heard everywhere—they almost brought Grandma to tears. She could envisage her own wedding. Even though it took place a short while after the war and her husband-to-be limped to the canopy, she remembered the tense silence in the synagogue as the wedding ceremony took place, and the elegant guests crowded around. Though some still carried the scars of the war, they were, wiping away a tear, all part of the awe encompassing the place as the bride and groom were joined in matrimony.

Grandma, and with her Grandpa, gradually withdrew into their own world. Though my parents kept going to visit them after their marriage, the encounters resembled a ceremony. The same words were always said, the same manners, like a group of people who feel they must maintain a process aimed at preserving itself. My parents asked about Grandpa's health, about how he occupied his time, about Grandma's job. She, for her part, inquired about the studies of her daughter and her husband, how they were supporting themselves, and after a while she inquired how the pregnancy was advancing.

I heard that when I was born Grandma lost her temper as she never had before. When my mother took me out of the hospital she placed me in an old braided basket a friend had given her. Grandma was shocked when she saw how the young baby was being carried, and for once in her life she screamed at my mom, shouting that she is irresponsible, this is no way to take care of a newborn baby. Mom was so taken by surprise when she saw her quiet, introverted mother shouting that she quickly removed me from the basket and placed me in the cradle Grandma had prepared in advance. By the way Mom talks about this incident it is clear that Grandma's harsh words are engraved in her memory, eroding the distance from her mother and betraying a need she had decided to abandon. She always added that the first days after the delivery, especially of a firstborn child, are very difficult, since everything is 'oversized'—the mother's body that still feels it is carrying a fetus, family relatives whose unfamiliar feelings make them lose their temper, and the young baby, which finds it hard to accept its removal from the hot, opaque bubble that surrounded it into the strong light and chilled air.

But after these harsh words Grandma returned to her moderate, restrained way. It was in her that Mom found support, so she says, since she never expected her to demonstrate so much excitement about the baby; in her way Grandma understood that more than anything my mom needed to be the sloppy, garrulous woman she was before I was born.

As a child I met Grandma every week. Already at the age of four or five I observed that she looked entirely different from my mom; in spite of her gray hair she seemed to me younger, more flexible. I thought that perhaps they pretended to be mother and daughter. I loved her elegant dresses, her slim figure, and the restrained way in which she approached me, purposely ignoring my young age and treating me without a touch of humor. When she inquired whether I wish to have animal- or vehicle-shaped cookies she waited patiently as I hesitated, and when I finally made up my mind and said I prefer cars she drew the cookies out of the jar and placed them in front of me on an elegant white plate. She took toasted bread and some cheese, placed them on a similar white plate, and sat beside me to dine together.

I've heard people say that even if a person overcomes childhood difficulties, as a parent they will emerge again. Angrily my mother watched me looking intensely at Grandma, examining every part of her appearance and trying to imitate her countenance. Though I was a naughty child, perhaps a bit cheeky, I never dared be forward with Grandma, I was always waiting for her to ask how I was. My mother found it hard to comprehend my fondness for her mother; she had given me a childhood full of freedom, without any manners, without any need to please anyone. She thought it was the most precious gift a mother could give her child. With great contempt she watched mothers setting their children's clothes right, or cleaning food residue around their mouth with a wrinkled handkerchief. And most of all she detested mothers who would tell their children openly not to be too loud, not to use inappropriate words, not to speak when adults are talking. She used to talk in a loud voice with her friends, almost shouting, and if someone looked at her with surprise, or even rebuke, she would stare back in a provocative and insulting manner.

But my strange development left Mom helpless. When I asked her at the age of five if she could buy me a dress like Grandma's dress, she looked at her sloppy shirt like a person before a mirror for the first time, seeing the reflection of a strange and distorted figure. She watched me and said nothing. I kept asking her when we would buy the dress, and she said 'when we get a chance'. But soon she realized that I was determined to look like Grandma and that she wouldn't be able to erase my childish wish. She tried to ask why I want a dress, saying it is uncomfortable to play in it and when I want to sit on the rug I would have to fold it under my legs. She even hinted that none of my friends have dresses—Grandma wears them because she is an elderly woman. Young girls don't dress this way. And where will we buy the dress?

Finally she decided to grant my wish. A mixture of restrained anger and clear thinking created a belief that satisfying the wish would make it meaningless. One day she returned home holding a blue dress with white buttons, with a belt zipped behind the back. The dress was too big, stretching under my knees; the belt was placed below the waist. But I put it on immediately and began walking like an elegant lady, taking small measured steps on the tips of my toes to conceal the unbecoming length of the dress.

The children at the nursery school watched me amazed, as if I was wearing a costume, and touched every part of the dress. And in spite of my young age I could see the hostile look of the teacher, although she quickly concealed it with a forced smile and a loud laugh. She whispered something to her assistant, who returned a whisper and a wink. I felt I was transparent and everyone was watching a blue dress with white buttons moving by itself, sometimes leaning against the nursery school walls, exhausted and embarrassed.

When Grandma came for a visit I hastened to put on the dress. She sat on an upright chair, let her hair down and then pulled it back behind her head, and asked for some cold water. The hot summer of Tel Aviv was exhausting: small sweat drops rolled down her high forehead but didn't melt her light makeup. Instinctively her hand ran through her hair, she straightened her dress and sat erect. I waited for a while and then stepped into the room, tall and festive, walking on the tips of my toes, looking straight at the wall without moving my head.

Grandma looked at me, smiled, and said quietly that the dress was very nice and becoming. But the dry, distant tone revealed utter indifference. I thought she was mocking me. To my surprise she then resumed the conversation with Mom, describing how hard the bus journey was on such a hot day. As she spoke she watched me again, but her gaze was joyless. I escaped to my room to hide my tears, and didn't come out until I heard she was going home. I didn't take off the dress; as I was called to say goodbye she stared at me coldly, almost with disappointment, and left.

Grandpa's death surprised us all. Though he was tall and thin, often working in their small garden, leaning to the ground, planting shrubs and flowers and uprooting weeds, apparently his heart was weak. One Saturday morning Grandma woke up and spoke to him. As he didn't answer, she touched him and immediately recoiled. His body was cold. Grandma had been a nurse during the war, so she could tell immediately he was dead. She lay in the bed beside him, motionless, absorbed by her heartbeats, which she felt could be heard from every part of her body. Even within her thin legs a huge drum sounded. Emptiness filled the room. Only after a couple of hours did she call an ambulance; and then her two daughters, to tell them that their father was dead.

Grandpa's friends came to his funeral, all old men dressed in suits, some using walking sticks with decorated heads, some accompanied by a spouse holding their arm, walking slowly in the cemetery, anxious and sad. Grandma walked with them, wearing a straight, black dress, her hair tied behind her head with a golden hairpin; I was afraid she would stumble and collapse. Her back a little bent, her gaze moved from one grave to another. Her mouth was slightly open, her jaws loose in a way that betrays weakness she had never had before. When we got to the grave she watched the covered body and her face turned gray, adopting the hue of the shroud wrapping Grandpa.

As the body was removed from the cart and cast into the grave my mom began to cry loudly, almost roaring. My aunt also wept, and the grandchildren looked at the two of them with amazement. Mom's loud wailing resembled an animal's voice, while her big body rattled with sobs; her sister grabbed her husband's arm, making a sound like a French horn. The weeping of the sisters continued while the undertakers threw dark brown clods of earth into the fresh grave, doing their job as though they were gardeners covering a new plant in a public park.

Grandma covered her face with a large white handkerchief. The straight nose and the big eyes vanished in the white cloth, looking soft and rounded through it. I thought her body was shivering slightly, but she leaned on no-one, standing both bent and straight. One of Grandpa's friends stepped forward and stood next to her, but she ignored the gesture, completely absorbed in the separation from Grandpa, which, during the burial process, was as mundane and terrestrial as one could imagine.

As a teenager I loved wandering through various neighborhoods of Tel Aviv. I often sneaked out of school and walked in shaded streets. Sometimes I would turn to the market in the southern part of the city, sometimes I walked along the seashore; eventually I found myself in the northern parts of Tel Aviv. And so one day, after a brisk walk of two hours, I was walking in the street where Grandma lived. I hesitated, unsure whether I should knock on her door. First I told myself that perhaps she is not home at this morning hour; but then I felt there was another reason for my hesitation. I was afraid that I would find Grandma neglected, shabby, lacking the straight posture and the sharp look, that if I surprised her I might find another figure, old and bent. Shamefully, I thought my mom would have liked me to see her that way. Curious and anxious, I stepped towards the door and rang the bell.

A gentle tone came through the door, and then the sharp feminine sound of approaching heels. Grandma opened the door, and with amazement and joy invited me in. She hugged me, but suddenly her face turned sober—*is something wrong?* I assured her everything was fine, and told her about my long walks during school hours. Grandma laughed and suggested I have something to eat. She brought a sweet-smelling cake and two cups of coffee, in the same white, bright plates of my childhood memories. After the excitement was over I examined her and realized she was as elegant as ever. Only her gray hair, now not pulled behind her head but flowing on her neck, emphasized the deep wrinkles set at the sides of her eyes and mouth. First we sat facing one another, sipping coffee and smiling. Grandma offered cake again and again, attempting to conceal the distance between us with motherly habits. She inquired about Mom, Dad, my sister, but in spite of my detailed report on each one of them the conversation was soon over, and it seemed there was nothing more to say.

She was silent for a while, and then she looked at me with concentration and asked: *what is your favorite subject in school?* The question took me by surprise because it was articulated simply and naturally, without pretense, with an almost childish desire to hear the answer. There was nothing didactic in her tone; she honestly wished to find out which subject I like. I answered: *geography, I really like geography.* At that very moment I realized how fond I was of this subject. Though I almost never prepared my homework and only rarely did well in the exams, my knowledge in this field exceeded that of all my classmates. My answer seemed to surprise her and she was wondering out loud *why geography?* I began with an apology: *I am not a good student and my grades are pretty mediocre.* Grandma moved her hand in a gesture of dismissal, and her face revealed total contempt; the grades are of no importance, the question is what it is that I find interesting. I commenced an explanation on the magic of maps, on hints of a different and enchanted world one could find in the brown spots with thin blue lines next to them, slitting continents their width and length. So are the green, coin-size stains, immense grazing areas, or those round points, lacking spatial features, denoting Rome, Paris, London.

Grandma was surprised by my detailed answer. She envisaged maps she had not seen since high school, a topographic map, a political map, a population map, a vegetation map: the entire world spread before her, and a touch of a hidden longing created a film of softness over her eyes. After a couple of minutes she moved her head from side to side, as if she had woken up, her hand ran through her hair and she pulled it behind her head, and then she asked me how exactly does one study geography.

I smiled and said that the most important tool is, of course, the atlas. I often review it. I also told her that on transparent papers I copied maps of states without writing their names, and then tested myself to see if I could tell where each one of them is. Grandma seemed a bit amused, but the touch of humor didn't stop her admiration: do I know where every country is? Even in Africa? Of course, I replied with pride, in each continent. She thought for a moment and then got up and announced that not far from her place there is an excellent bookstore; we would go there immediately and buy a grand atlas, brand new, with all the various types of maps.

After this I often visited Grandma. When I told my mom about it she seemed disturbed and gloomy. She sat on the swinging chair on the porch, a large woman wearing a man's shirt and huge cotton pants, her feet dark and coarse, looking at me as though I carried a riddle she couldn't solve. She inquired what we talk about, but I hesitated to describe our conversations. Grandma was willing to drift anywhere, to hear anything; she took an interest in stories of distant, remote places, but also in my daily life, my friends and classmates.

One day I arrived at her house upset and agitated. My best friend, whom I had known since elementary school, had begun dating my ex-boyfriend. Even though I left him because he was inclined to elaborate on events that took place a long time ago and immerse himself in details I couldn't understand, I was infuriated by their relationship. I got to Grandma's place angry and insulted. She was glad to see me, but immediately noticed my sullen look and my forced smile that vanished quickly. She inquired why I was angry. I told her at length and in detail about their dates, how I found out by chance, how my friend told me nothing about it, how she betrayed our friendship; and I told her of my immense anger, which I didn't know how to ease or contain.

Grandma looked at me almost in wonder. For a moment I thought she was concealing a smile, but I examined her carefully and found no hint of amusement. Her face seemed somewhat wrinkled, the skin of the neck reddish, the vivid eyes focusing on me and wishing to understand something, struggling to overcome an obstacle but failing to do so. *Why does it make you so mad,* she asked, *you say you have no interest in this boy, you admit that if they had known each other before he met you, you would have thought them suitable for each other.*

Overwhelming fury filled me, a wrath that could be overcome only with an immense effort. Why doesn't she understand? Once again, my admiration of Grandma turned into a sour disappointment. I came to her believing she would support me, but I was wrong. I recalled mom's anger as she spoke of Grandma, and now I fully comprehended it. Despair at her answers, distant and rational, blurred the boundaries. Against my better judgment I accused her, *you don't understand, she has been my best friend ever since I was a kid, we shared everything, it is a terrible betrayal, I don't know what to do, I want to call her and cry until I remember that I can't.* And then, in a muffled voice that crept from within me, I heard myself saying *I understand why mom doesn't discuss anything with you, you understand nothing*. Already then, in spite of the shouting and accusations, I couldn't help observing that the intense look in her eyes transformed into pain. She looked at me and said nothing; I felt her face was melting away. Immediately I was sorry for what I had said. Grandma stretched out a bony hand and removed the plates from the table, walking erectly to the kitchen. I got up and went towards the door. As I turned around to say goodbye she stood at the entrance of the kitchen and looked at me. For a moment I was certain that tears filled her eyes and that her chin was jerking strangely. But she stifled everything, I could almost hear her self-reproach; she said *goodbye* and turned to her room.

I decided to walk home and not to take the bus. Walking conquers any outburst, tones down every fear; the monotonous pace overcomes any emotion and adapts it to a constant, unchanging rhythm. Even though I knew I would have to walk for an hour and a half, I simply couldn't stand or sit down. At first I thought it was a mistake to expect someone of her age to sympathize with a girl of my age. But then I had to admit I was mistaken, in other matters Grandma understood me very well. Again I envisaged the relationship between my friend and the ex-boyfriend; it brought back the blinding and enervating anger. I imagined them together, wishing to deepen the pain, to prove to myself how profound was the betrayal. Yet after long minutes of walking the anger turned somewhat bothersome. The need to be loyal to a justified emotion became harder, their combined figures gradually became blurred, the contours were left but the colors faded and the facial features disappeared.

Again I thought about Grandma. Her penetrating eyes, filled with tears, were now more vivid than the figures of my friend and her boyfriend. Why can't she understand? All the way I thought about her reaction, breaking it into words and then reconstructing the sentences, which seemed obscure and strange. Even when the anger had subsided I couldn't comprehend them. I found it hard to believe that she was disregarding my emotions, but I couldn't understand her aloof and remote stand.

After about two months I came to visit her again. I knocked lightly on the door, and facing her radiating and inviting eyes I stepped in hesitantly, on the tips of my toes, as if I was hoping that my presence wouldn't become a burden. Once again the elegant plates and the decorated mugs were drawn out, an odor of steaming coffee filled the kitchen, and on the table Grandma put fresh cookies, as if they were kept there especially for me. She asked how all the family members were doing; it was as though I had never lost my temper and said such biting words.

After a couple of minutes we were silent. Grandma cleaned the table, putting away the plates and pushing the chairs into their places. I was appalled by the thought I would leave as a stranger, as if we had never talked about so many things. I kept sitting, ignoring how everything around me was turning clean, and finally I said quietly 'I am sorry'. Grandma seemed surprised, apparently she thought I wouldn't mention our quarrel. She put down the cloth and sat down beside me, looking at me but absorbed in her thoughts. Her fingers, sliding back and forth on the table, seemed almost deformed. I was wondering how they would look without the rings; they had become part of her body, it was impossible to imagine her without them.

Grandma opened with an apology—she was sorry she had offended me, in no way had she meant to belittle my feelings. She always respected me and took care not to insult me. She doesn't understand why I was so angry. She remembers my mom used to be angry with her exactly like that when she was my age. And regarding the friend who betrayed me, she finds it impossible to comprehend the deep emotional turmoil this relationship provokes. Not that she can't understand how profound love can be, almost enslaving, but this is not the case here. This is a relationship she finds hard to define—reliant on friendship, a dependency, perceiving the friend as part of oneself and not as a separate entity. She is very sorry, she can't find the right words, but something about this friendship exceeds the realm of a relationship between two people and is really about perceiving oneself. She finds it difficult to grasp why this betrayal is so insulting if I don't like this boy at all. It seems to her that what I find distressing is the disengagement from the friend; I find the independent stand uncomfortable. The dependency on this friend blurs my vision, prevents me from seeing the distorted nature of this friendship. And by the way, this is not the first time she has seen this since she came to Israel. And as a matter of fact, what exactly am I mad at? What did my friend betray? The loyalty of two young girls, hiding in the deep forest and swearing that forever-forever they would be friends? She is sorry, she says it with pain, but what was offended here is a part of me that doesn't want to exist independently, but desperately needs to rely on others.

I was speechless. I had never heard her speak so bluntly; even her voice, which was always quiet, turned harsh. I thought she was shivering a bit. I looked at her and saw a touch of bitterness. The seclusion within the small community of immigrants from England, the habits that seemed so detached, the abyss between herself and her daughters, they all created a grudge she concealed well. But now she seemed determined to ignore all inhibitions or barriers. One could imagine that the things she told me had been voiced earlier in the room, even though there was no one there but herself, in a whisper or out loud. We stood a couple of minutes facing one another, upset and silent. Finally I kissed her and left.

When I got home I decided to talk to my friend. I felt something was impaired, but I didn't know what it was. Clearly the chance that her words would restore our friendship was slim, but more than anything I was driven by curiosity to find out where exactly was the rupture that I was so eager to heal. I called to say that I would like to speak to her, and she invited me to her house home. As I got there she was waiting at the door, smiling as if I were a relative returning from a long journey who should be greeted in a way that demonstrated how she was missed. Refusing food and drink, I was invited to her room, so familiar yet now tidy and clean: the clothes which had always been scattered on the floor were gone, the bed was covered with a nice bedspread, and even the desk was shining. My friend sat smiling on the bed and began to explain how happy she was that we can be friends again, and that her relationship with this boy won't stand between us. Anyway I didn't want him, so why do I care if they are dating now? I am her best friend, she can't speak with anyone the way she does with me, we could spend time together —and she heard some very interesting gossip she wished to share with me.

I looked at her, swinging her bare feet and running a long finger through her curls, her eyes inviting and enigmatic, her smile sweet, and wondered what had gone wrong. Grandma was right, I was entirely indifferent to this boy; thinking about the both of them suddenly seemed ridiculous and senseless. My friend began talking about another girl, trying to make her story funny and engaging. I smiled at her, but besides a couple of familiar names I heard nothing. It was as if a huge, heavy door was slammed in my face: I am shocked by the loud slam shaking the entire house, there is no way to reopen it, I comprehend it in a flash, but since I am eager to remove any doubt I keep pushing it, but it is massive and can't be moved. I said goodbye to my friend—I promised I would come again— and hastily left her house.

Everything came loose, nothing was properly fastened. Of course the friendship ended, there was no room for so many words in a years-long intimacy. My visits to other friends were rushed, and I often left abruptly, almost without saying goodbye. I walked for long hours along the shore, from the south of the city northward, and then back to the south. The sea was almost always completely flat, the coast shallow and transparent. But sometimes I saw steep waves, breaking far from the shore and drifting back into deep, invisible undercurrents.

Geography studies at the university turned out to be a total disappointment. Already from the first class I was immersed in endless technical terms, describing natural phenomena in a quantitative way entirely alien to windy summits, wide rivers crossing old cities, and broad oceans. At first I told myself there is no way of reaching these places without knowing them in detail, each fact evaluated and related to other facts. But soon I felt it was a limited path, with no prospect of transcending heat-struck, sweaty Tel Aviv, where even in the fall the sun is blazing until a late evening hour.

I decided to ask Grandma for advice. Though I met her only once every couple of months, I could talk to her in a language comprehensible to both of us. One afternoon when I went to her, Grandma stood before me erect and thin, but looking somewhat fatigued; her face seemed to sag, and suddenly I saw the resemblance between her and my mom. Once again the elegant plates were drawn out and the smell of freshly-ground coffee filled the kitchen. She served brown, glossy cookies, and asked how everyone was. After all her questions were answered, she waited patiently to hear in what matter her advice was needed.

I began with a description of the Geography studies; I tried to describe them as accurately as possible, like a person asking for an expert's advice, portraying the circumstances in a way that wouldn't affect an impartial judgment. The professors teach the material very well, the students are pleasant; I don't know why but I was expecting something else, I thought the courses would focus on different issues. Grandma looked at me in deep concentration, absorbed by every word as if it was being said in a foreign language which she had just begun to study. Finally, with a clear effort, she asked what exactly was I expecting? I blushed, I couldn't conceal my embarrassment, and said *I don't really know.* I looked down and added very quietly that I am eager to go beyond my world, to move from life in Israel to other places, or rather, to other realms. I don't know why but I feel there is something confining about my daily routine and I had hoped—I can see how strange it sounded—that geography studies would be liberating, would unbind me, granting me—well, a free life.

Grandma smiled softly, without any ridicule. She thinks she understands me, but she is not sure. She wasn't sure what she would study, but her life circumstances made her give up education altogether. Though she was a nurse during the war she had no formal education, and she didn't want to take care of others all her life. Grandpa was an engineer, but she had to admit that in spite of the intimacy between them, when it came to professional matters they were completely estranged. She could never figure out the sketches he made, yet he thought they were extremely beautiful. When she came to Israel she was hoping to study at the university but the need to adapt quickly to an unfamiliar language and the strange environment discouraged her. She often wondered what would have happened had she stayed in England; she thinks she would have acquired a professional degree, perhaps she would have been a lawyer. And by the way, when I say 'free life'—what exactly do I mean? Somehow, when she looks at me, she also feels that my life is affected by so many constraints and she has to admit she fails to understand most of them.

I looked at Grandma, her huge eyes squinting with effort and concentration; she brought her head close to mine, as if I was about to reveal a secret, to whisper it in her ear, and she didn't want to miss a single word. Now I see her face is full of wrinkles, the hair behind the head is all white. She stretched a twisted hand, held my hand softly, caressed it gently as if it was fragile, and waited. Her anticipation that I would say something was distressing, so I tried to explain again: I am not sure how to describe it, I also find it strange, but she, Grandma, seems freer than me. Her experiences seem to me so different from my own, almost remote. What does it mean 'remote' she asks. I don't know, sometimes I feel as if I am caught in a whirlpool while she is managing her life. Everything about her life is so different from mine—the clothing, the jewelry, the friends, the house, the beautiful plates, it all adds up to a whole fully distinct from its surroundings, whereas my life is too interwoven with my environment. She squints even harder, she seems too alert, a bit nervous, and then she asks me: does my mom feel the same? I am confused, I don't understand what she has to do with it, but I answer anyway: no, mom likes to spend time with friends more than anything, she detests any seclusion, she thinks it is a defect that must be fixed. Grandma taps on the table with her fingers—I have never seen her so tense—and wonders aloud: but isn't it good to be part of your environment? Why does it bother you? No, Grandma, I answer, not like this, not when you can't see the distance between yourself and the others anymore, and every inner space is conquered through an exhaustive and discouraging struggle.

Dori approached me with a question about a book he was looking for; I was the senior librarian during the evening hours. From the very start there was something unclear about him—a tall, thin man, with large, amber-colored eyes, dressed in a somewhat old-fashioned manner, there was no knowing whether his gaze was shy or cunning. He addressed me in a practical tone, almost complaining: perhaps I could help him find books on the development of urbanization in Israel and in Europe? He has been wandering around the library for almost an hour and can't find the right bookshelf. But after I began searching the catalog and looking for books on this subject, he started to apologize, saying he is a journalist for a respectable newspaper and is preparing an article on the development of cities in

Israel, and needs assistance finding material. He is sorry, he had already asked the advice of two librarians and had almost given up. The first directed him to the wrong bookshelf and the other one asked since when journalists are interested in books?

Dori began coming to the library often and finally he dared to invite me for dinner at his place. He lived in the southern part of Tel Aviv, on the second floor of a shabby apartment building, facing a tall eucalyptus tree. The walls of his apartment were covered with dark brown bookshelves, dusted and gloomy, filled with old books. However, the décor looked like a young student's place, with printed fabrics covering the walls, a Chinese umbrella hanging down from the ceiling; at the center of the room stood a red sofa, heavily stained. For dinner the dining table was covered with an oversized tablecloth that almost touched the floor on both sides. Dori served the food excitedly. His old-fashioned clothes were stained from cooking, but he didn't notice it since he was completely absorbed by the sights and sounds emerging from the oven. I recalled that my mother used to cook this way—splattering drops of oil and food all over the kitchen, but fully focused on the ingredients losing their shape and texture and slowly turning into a prepared dish.

After we were done eating Dori expected compliments on his cooking and I hastened to praise the various dishes. Exactly like my mother, after the meal he sank into the big armchair, took off his shoes and stretched his feet forward. First he closed his eyes, then he opened them and stared at me; it was unclear whether he was looking at me like a young boy in love or as a mature man seducing yet one more girl. I smiled at him but he remained grave. Finally he said, in an almost blunt tone, that he wished I would stay for the night.

Nothing is more distressing than a daily routine created between lovers. After the accelerated heartbeats, the scent of an unfamiliar body, adopting strange memories, comes a morning in which one has to hurry to work and quickly take care of overdue tasks.

Dori leaped out of bed as the alarm went off, paced nervously between the bathroom and the kitchen, and after a couple of minutes I heard the door slam. I was left alone in the wide bed. I lay motionless, and after long minutes I decided to visit Grandma.

When she opened the door I realized I had woken her up. She wore a shining gray robe and fleecy slippers; her eyes were struggling with the bright daylight as she attempted to conceal her late morning sleep. Her half-closed eyes and the gray, disheveled hair made her look strange and I thought that it was impossible from her face to tell whether it was a man or a woman. Grandpa's face surfaced from her eyes: Grandma looked at me exactly as he would have, with skeptical curiosity, and invited me in. She walked slowly to the kitchen and turned on the coffee machine, which began to gurgle and steam. Finally the machine spat hot coffee, Grandma put toasted bread and butter on a plate, and invited me to join her for breakfast.

I am not sure why but I found her negligent look upsetting. A kind of anger took over. I was sorry I came to visit her but I didn't want to leave immediately, so as not to offend her. She seemed to feel nothing and as usual began inquiring about my parents, my sister, my job. After I reported everything in detail I said quietly, almost in a whisper, that I have a boyfriend.

A young, mischievous gaze popped out of the old face. Grandma straightened, tied her hair behind her head, and fastened the robe's belt, as if she was facing a wonderful adventure. She smiled, waited for a while, and then asked me to tell her about him. I tried to describe Dori accurately, without complimenting him too much or stressing his faults. Grandma was so attentive I felt she could hardly breathe. And as I completed the description she looked at me softly, almost in a way one would look at a newborn baby, with both adoration and deep anxiety.

She got up and announced she would get dressed immediately and we would go shopping, she would buy me a present, perhaps a garment. After a couple of minutes I heard the tapping of her heels approaching. She appeared, elegant as ever, her white hair shining; it matched perfectly with the grey dress, decorated in red and orange. With a determined expression she held my arm, suggesting that I follow her. We went outside, walked in narrow, shaded alleys until we got to a small dress shop, almost invisible, at the old shopping center. Grandma opened the door and was welcomed warmly. Apparently both the dressmaker and her assistant knew her well.

The assistant stared at me with utter bewilderment, gazing at my faded jeans and black Tee shirt and then looking puzzled at Grandma. Am I accompanying her? Grandma smiled and said I am her granddaughter and she wishes to buy me a dress. With a forced smile the dressmaker hinted something with a glance to the assistant and said something in a foreign language; they spoke about me like a doctor and nurse examining a patient, not wanting to reveal the gravity of her condition, attempting to conceal the small but oppressive details of her disease.

The dressmaker got up from her chair behind the sewing machine, walked towards me and stared at me for a couple of moments as if I was naked—calculating my body measurements, walking around me to see me from the front, from behind, from the side, estimating my height and weight, lingering on every flaw. Finally she turned to Grandma and said she has a couple of dresses that might fit me. She drew a curtain covering one wall—behind it a door was revealed—disappeared and returned with a pile of clothes.

The dresses were spread out in the small room; the abundance of shapes and colors filled the little store completely. Small red and blue squares were covered with large green circles, black triangles and squares on a white fabric spilled over tiny, purple summer flowers, a glossy pink cloth poured on a slightly wrinkled Indian fabric, which fell on endless violet orange and red stripes set against a pale background. But the charm was abruptly disrupted when I heard the sour voice of the assistant asking Grandma which cut would best suit me. Grandma drew out one dress, white with thin blue lines, and asked me to try it on.

A strange woman is looking at me from the mirror: young, with light hair, her eyes wide open, her rounded body visible through the dress, which fits her figure well; she is looking at me skeptically, but a light twitch on her face resembles a smile; her body seems somewhat tight, almost strained, though she is standing still. After a couple of moments in which she stands motionless, she finally begins to move, examining the feminine body from different angles and then she sees that another figure is reflected in the mirror. Her grandmother is looking at her with a resolute gaze, her eyes dark, almost black, and she is waiting quietly and patiently for the spark of a smile to transform into full, clear satisfaction.

I want the dress—I heard my voice loud and determined. Again the dressmaker and her assistant exchanged words in a foreign language, and then turned to Grandma and asked if I wished to purchase another dress. She shook her head, so they picked up all the other dresses and disappeared with them through the secret door. When they returned, the assistant suggested she would wrap the dress, but I declared I had no intention of taking it off. With apparent disgust, they put my jeans and black tee shirt in a shopping bag and placed it at the entrance of the store.

When I met Dori in the evening I tried to look casual. I came to his place late at night, climbed the dark stairway, and rang the doorbell. Dori opened the door and leaned on it, his face pale and exhausted. After a long day of hard work he had come home tired, and more than anything he wanted to lie down on the red sofa and fall asleep. Once in a long while he would wake after a couple of hours and move to the bed, but usually he would relax on the sofa and sleep until morning. And indeed, the sofa had adopted the contour of his body: a long valley crossed it, ending in a crushed pillow. But despite his tired countenance, a glint of light flashed in his eyes when he saw me wearing the new dress. He examined me openly, as if I was a stranger. I was expecting a smile, some compliments, but he seemed distant, gazing at me covetously but unfriendly, his eyes following the dress's curves as though they were a knight's armor that had to be ripped apart in order to conquer him. I am a bit frightened, Dori suddenly looks so different, the pleasant manners are gone, along with the soft, polite language; he is not trying to make it easy for me, to avoid the embarrassment—on the contrary, he is not leaning on the door anymore but standing erect, pulling me towards him, and behind my shoulder I feel heavy, strained breathing.

Dori and I are sitting on a balcony facing the sea. At this late evening hour the sun can't be seen, but the red gleam is still there beyond the horizon, spreading golden dust in the sky. The sea is dark blue, almost black, reflecting nothing but darkness. We both look down at the table. I fold my arms firmly and Dori's hands clasp the corners of the table. My teeth are biting my lips and Dori is swallowing an invisible drink. Can I manage not to cry until I leave? Should I go now? I will never return here, perhaps I should linger for a while. But the tears, still held back, will soon slide onto my cheeks, so I decide to go. As I walk towards the door Dori sits motionless, avoids looking at me, his gaze is focused on the cracked plastic table.

The stairway is dirty and musty. I find it hard to breathe the foul odor, and hasten to get out to the street. Perhaps he sees me from the balcony but I don't turn my head upwards. I stop a taxi and asked to be taken home. The taxi begins to drive and I sit stunned, trying to reconstruct the words, Dori's face, but everything appears as if behind a screen of smoke. Suddenly I feel weak. I find it hard to sit—perhaps I will lie down in the back seat—I don't know how I will manage to get out of the cab and walk home. My head is so heavy, I must rest it against the window. The taxi is driving northward along the shore and then turns east. But as it approaches my place, I realize I won't be able to stay alone for one single moment. I have been living with Dori for several months now, and my apartment was left almost empty. When the taxi comes to a stop, I ask the driver to take me to Grandma's address.

She opens the door and her face reveals alarm: why am I so pale? I look as if I am about to faint. Am I sick? She will call the doctor immediately. I make an effort to reach the sofa, take off my shoes, and lie on it. I sprawl on my back, my limbs spread, one foot on the floor, the other on the armrest, my head drops behind the seat and my hands are placed at my side. Grandma is in a panic; I watch her rushing to the phone, dialing and waiting for an answer. But then the tears burst and can't be halted, I feel their warmth on my face but I am too weak to wipe them. Grandma looks at me, puts down the receiver and rushes towards me. She crouches on the floor and embraces me, her kisses on my cheeks washing away the tears.

I've been staying with Grandma for a couple of days now. In Grandpa's room there is a comfortable bed on which he used to rest in the afternoon after long hours of sketching plans. Grandma put on new, shining white bedspreads with a pleasant lavender smell. I don't know whether the nice odor eases my pain or deepens it. I am awake at night, turning in bed, struggling with a void that fills me. I spend the days with Grandma, sharing her daily routine: a walk to the nearby grocery store, from there to the pharmacy, and back home. I never knew she had so many acquaintances. Almost all of them speak English or German, they are always happy to see her and she introduces me with obvious pride. During lunch we listen to the BBC World Service news broadcast, and then rest for a while. In the afternoon I go with Grandma to the public library.

She exchanges books and meets friends—I see she has beaus. An elderly man in an elegant suit escorts her, telling bad, boring jokes, and making her put on an amused expression. And there is also a nice English-speaking gentleman who kisses her hand every time he meets her. She treats them kindly but doesn't stop to chat.

I borrowed two books from the library, but I can't read. After a couple of paragraphs my thoughts wander and I put down the book; I don't even put the bookmark in the right place. Though I constantly think of Dori's words about love that is detached from daily life, I know they are empty and hollow and that it is pointless to keep thinking about them. But the hope that a new insight might remove the despair makes me remember every word, every expression. I have turned into a young, deserted child: like a toddler exiled from her home, she is standing outside the house and watching the closed gate expectantly, torn between a desire to bear the insult with pride and disappear and the need to scream in panic and fear and beg to be allowed in. But the two wishes are perfectly counterbalanced—she is crying in front of the gate, refusing to leave but not asking to return home.

Grandma is watching me without saying anything. I know she is following my gestures and expressions, but I prefer to ignore this. There is no point in asking her to stop, at most she will try to conceal her inquisitiveness. At first she suggested we have coffee somewhere or go to a movie, but I refused. Afterwards she asked if I could help her with the house maintenance. I know there is no need for that, Grandma always managed the household wisely and efficiently. I replied without hesitation that when I have time I will help. She smiled and nodded. Once in a while I hear her speaking with mom on the phone, telling her about my daily routine. She has an apologetic tone, I don't know why. Perhaps mom is angry that I am staying with Grandma and not with her, or perhaps she dislikes the way Grandma treats me.

A couple of days ago mom came for a visit. She sank into the huge armchair, breathing heavily from walking and also from her rapid speaking. In spite of her anecdotes about family members, it is clear she is embarrassed and a bit scared. She sees my pain but doesn't know what to say. She has been used to sharing life's upheavals with friends, the long conversations providing some comfort. She is wondering why I don't do the same, but she knows she can't force a dialogue. She is eager to talk about me and Dori, why we were attracted to each other and why we broke up, but she dares say nothing. The worry makes her look contemplative, almost sad. In spite of her big body and sloppy clothes she seems to me younger, somehow girlish. They both watch me, Grandma with a distant sadness and mom with obvious pain and embarrassment, their faces revealing helplessness and despair.

It's been a couple of months since I moved in with Grandma. This morning I acceded to her requests to stay at home and spend some time with her. I slept late, and then we decided to have breakfast at a nearby café. In spite of the thin rain we left home; just as we got there the rain began pouring on the pavement. We sat at a small table next to the window and watched the drops splashing everywhere. As coffee and cakes were served, Grandma began talking. She asked me about my job at the library, inquired about my friends, told me about encounters with writers, and, very much unlike her usual way, expressed some fierce political opinions. It was the twisted development of the conversation, the fluent shift from one subject to another, which made me think she was aiming for something. In a casual manner she said that she had met someone she knew a long time ago, Grandpa's friend from London; they hardly recognized each other since they hadn't seen each other for so many years. He told her he came to Israel about ten years after her and that for many years now he has been the Middle East correspondent for a well-known British newspaper. Even now, at his advanced age, he writes almost every day, but he is looking for young people to assist him and eventually to take his place.

Watching me carefully, Grandma says she thinks I am suitable for the job, and if I want it I would be accepted immediately. I am surprised, speechless. Me? The insult is overpowering. I give a short laugh. Grandma thinks my condition is so poor that she is driven to suggest preposterous things. I look at her with hostility, but she doesn't let go. She grasps my hand with her bony hands decorated with rings, stares at me and says I need to start something new, to discover a new aspect of life. I had always written well and this would be a chance to get into a new field with many opportunities. I remind her that I am a librarian but her face remains unchanged, as if I had said nothing. I have no words, the offer is ridiculous, insulting, Grandma doesn't acknowledge my talents but my failure, and this attempt is like giving ballerina shoes to an invalid woman.

She lets go of my hand and silence falls on us. I crumble what is left of the cake, looking down at the table. I would have liked to get up and walk away but I sit hunched over, moving the crumbs back and forth on the table. Finally I begin to feel uncomfortable; I dare to look at Grandma. The palms of her hands on the table are dark and spotted, her neck sags, her makeup no longer manages to conceal her age. Then I look at her eyes and see they are filled with tears. Transparent drops drip on her cheek, and she takes a white, fragrant handkerchief to wipe them off.

I stretch out my hand towards her. Grandma is indifferent to the panic her tears create. She holds me with a slightly shivering hand. The makeup that melted around her eyes makes her look somewhat clownish, for a moment I think she is wearing a white mask with black and blue eyes. But her solemn expression and the strained look overshadow the blending colors, she lowers her voice and says, *enough, let go of the insult, you are wearing it as if it was a long warm coat and you are unwilling to take it off even on hot summer days. Let it go, it doesn't protect you but only makes you a heavy, clumsy woman.* I answer that it is not easy to ignore an insult that is born of love; I can't take Dori's words, his reservation, our break-up. Skeptically she looks at me for a moment, her eyes are roaming the room, and then she says *again you are looking for support, but this time you are clinging to pain. Again you are leaning on love and friendship, only here it is about the lack of them. Time and again another person becomes part of you and not a separate entity; here it is the absence of Dori. If you had stayed his partner you would have become his shadow, a mirror reflecting his life. Dori is sinking into you, you are looking at yourself through his eyes, examining yourself and finding so many faults. Get rid of him, you don't need him. When will you finally see yourself through your own eyes? Believe me, you will see many shapes and colors you never knew existed, and you will see yourself like you never did before.*

I am weak, a dreadful weariness overtakes me I would like to answer Grandma but I don't have enough strength. I want to go home but I feel I wouldn't be able to walk. A kind of sadness is developing slowly, first only a hint, more like a light gloom, but gradually it transforms into emptiness mixed with despair. I drop a sugar bag and it falls on the floor; I don't stretch my hand to pick it up. Grandma arches her eyebrows and twists her mouth in reproach, and says, *I understand the sense of loss, relying on others is very comfortable, and sometimes very satisfying. But be careful, because it is so tempting one doesn't see the trap.*

Suddenly a slashing rain came down on the roof of the café, so noisy that everyone fell silent and looked up. It felt as if the ceiling would collapse from the sudden weight of water running on it. Grandma and I did not speak. She held a handkerchief and turned it over and over in her hand, immersed in her thoughts and looking at no one, absorbed by what seemed a bitter disappointment. I found the silence embarrassing: conversation with Grandma was usually so fluent, but today, uncharacteristically she said nothing; as though she was alone.

After a couple of minutes of uneasiness I mustered some courage and asked her how come she finds no support in other people.

She looked like a person awaking from a deep sleep. First she watched the rain beyond the window and didn't respond. Then she turned to me, paused for a while, and said she was born and raised in a different place, in another world; she didn't know how different it was until she came to Israel. And no, she doesn't mean the landscape, though Tel Aviv was once arid, but the unclear relations between people. In fact, no, this is not the issue. She can't find the exact words but the core of it is the way people perceive themselves. Yes, she knows these are vague, obscure words, but these notions had always been part of her, ever since she came to Israel. She is not sure what the problem is exactly, she has been trying to articulate it in full for many years but never quite succeeded. Did she talk to anyone about it? Yes, with Grandpa. He understood exactly what she meant, implicitly, without spelling it out. She once asked him what he thought about it. He burst into laughter and said that native Israelis remind him of puppies detached from their mother, they have to try and guess how she would have raised them; but the absence of the mother makes them try to find support in each other, though this intimacy is not helpful at all. *But we left our home in Europe*, she tried to object, *yes*, he answered smiling, *but we grew up in the bosom of a mother who shaped us, even if we left her.*

The waitress approached and began clearing the table. She placed the mugs on the plates, and then removed them. The tablecloth was a little stained and Grandma kept looking at the stain. She was silent again, and I was thinking about what she had said. Though her words were obscure, they had a familiar echo. Something about the constant need to guess how one should behave, the lack of solid posts supporting everyday life made sense, though it was not fully intelligible. I couldn't come up with an example, but still the lack of a well-defined pattern seemed to describe my life very well.

The rain became heavier and again the sound of water falling on the glass ceiling filled the café. Dusky clouds covered the sky, darkening the early afternoon light. Thick drops dripped on the window, transforming into long streams falling on the pavement. Outside, a woman carrying bags ran clumsily, looking for shelter from the rain soaking her coat. A bus passing in the street left a water trail splattering on the pavement.

Grandma looked at the heavy rain, and I thought she was drowning in her memories. Perhaps she was thinking of the light English rain? Her foreignness was so obvious, so touching. I don't know why tears came into my eyes; I forced myself not to embrace her, to bring her close to me. A woman who had lived most of her life in a strange place, spending time only with European friends, and after Grandpa died being left so lonely. I am sure some people looked at her with ridicule, perhaps even made fun of her openly. Even her own daughters conducted themselves so differently from her. I held her hand softly and said,

'I am sorry.'

I was expecting a light smile admitting the difficulties, a sad look, perhaps even a hug of closeness. But to my utter surprise Grandma burst into a loud, almost vulgar, laugh, and then, immediately, feeling it was an extreme exhibition of emotions, she began to speak quietly. *Sorry? Why?* It is the other way around. Throughout the years she lived in Israel she felt her character better fits life here than that of native Israelis. As a matter of fact she thinks that had she grown up here she would have found it hard to lead a proper life. The distance embedded in her, a sense of self-value that doesn't derive from her place in society, is what makes her life more free and happy. Though she loves Israel dearly and she and Grandpa made it their home, their life was essentially that of a man and a woman, somewhat detached from their environment. Not that she hadn't experienced many insults, she had heard them clearly, since native Israelis, men in particular, think it possible to giggle at a woman's face without her taking notice. And the endless insinuations regarding her being a foreigner, about her lack of understanding, the underestimation of her, it was all evident and clear, but still it was better this way. There is no place where a structured lifestyle is needed more, with well-defined habits that are never questioned. She is looking at the people closest to her, even her beloved daughters, and sometimes she feels their life is conditioned, they constantly shape their daily routine, and she thinks it is an exhausting effort; growing into a pattern of life bestows much stability and peace, like a pathway whose length and width are predetermined, and you can either leap through it joyfully or walk head bent forward, absorbed in contemplation.

Grandma drew out the handkerchief and began wiping her face. She completely removed the remains of her makeup and her face was now utterly clear. Though her age was fully visible, her face had a fresh brightness, like a luster outshining the thin wrinkles. She let her hair down and then tied it behind her head with the golden pin, straightened her dress, sat erect on the chair, and ordered another cup of coffee. After putting the handkerchief back in her purse she gave a small smile and said quietly that she thought that I, more than any of our family members, would understand what she was saying. Why? Isn't this the reason why I was visiting her for years, examining every detail of her life as if it was a chapter in a textbook that has to be memorized, wondering how I could adopt her way of life? Ever since I was small she saw an exploring look on my face, but childish naiveté made me think that it was the dresses that I should imitate. But once I grew up, it became clear that I really wanted to resemble her, at least in certain respects. She loves me dearly, I know this very well, yet she sees me clearly: I am looking for a way out of what seems to her like a labyrinth, curved roads that criss-cross each other.

I was surprised by her candor; she had never spoken about our friendship. Now a certain shell had cracked, and something new emerged. Grandma deserted her motherly tone and spoke to me in a different, more direct manner. I also sat erect, straightened my hair and looked outside. The rain had stopped and the clouds were lighter and brighter. Gentle sunlight filtered in once in a while, and the street seemed perfectly clean, the pavements dark and wet and the trees slowly shedding water from their leaves. I may have been alarmed by her words but I also felt somewhat pleased. They had a friendly tone, a new melody, like an accordion playing a popular tune. The sentences came one after the other, almost neutrally, with neither ridicule nor extra softness.

Grandma crossed her hands and smiled slightly. Her face had a soft orange tone of sunrays emerging from behind a cloud after the rain. She waited a bit to see if I was about to answer her, but as she saw I was steeped in thoughts she turned to me in a low voice and asked me to reconsider the job offer. I should think about it seriously, she said, since she believes it would be a golden opportunity, and that it carried benefits beyond professional life. The job at the library is far from exciting, I have to admit that. She understands that I find the closeness to books comfortable, and studious people come to the library. But I don't fulfill my potential there, just sink into a comfortable routine. She feels this comfort is a huge obstacle, a block that must be bypassed. And since Dori and I had broken up, even the routine had become irksome, so I should get rid of it, start something new. She thinks writing would have many benefits, it would make me articulate my thoughts clearly, remove the eyes of others which emerge every time I describe something, and an independent perspective would take their place. And further, it is the foreign press, not Israeli, and the need to describe Israeli reality to readers who are unfamiliar with it might well refine the perception, enhance the personal tone. She is hoping that I would avoid any clichés; in any case they persuade no one. The description must be as rich as possible, illustrating how complex life is here, but still pointing to the main facts. She is absolutely sure I will be an excellent journalist, if fact she finds it surprising that I have never taken any interest in this occupation. I don't have the right personality for this? She doesn't understand what I mean. The job will be mine if I want it, her childhood friend would prefer me to anyone else. And regarding the work itself, she thinks what is needed most is talent. Embarrassing details are unnecessary; the point is an extensive portrayal of daily life here. And by the way, she had already told the friend about me, and he was expecting my call.

Grandma fears I will be angry since she approached him without asking me first, but I don't care. I don't know why but I feel a deep urge to satisfy myself. Perhaps I will purchase a new set of earrings. A childish spirit overtakes me—I almost order sweet cocoa and a chocolate cake with cream. Grandma looks at me somewhat amazed, for she is talking about work and I am indifferent and smiling slightly. Do I suddenly look cheerful? True, I feel this way, though I'm not sure why. Maybe because of the clean wind after the heavy rain or perhaps because once again I have plans, even if only for the next few hours. *What plans? To buy a couple of things. No thanks, Grandma, I want to buy them by myself. Why? I am not sure, I think there is a special pleasure in satisfying your own desires, ignoring everyone else. You will approve of anything I choose? I am sure, Grandma, you are the best person to shop with, but this time I will go alone. Maybe I want to try myself to see if I can pick the thing you would have bought.*

We pick our way carefully between the crowded tables and leave the café. Grandma is in front of me, erect as always but she is finding it a bit hard to walk, pausing before every step. I am careful not to rush her, although I want to say goodbye and leave. When we are finally outside the coffee shop she looks at me questioningly. I smile, run my hand through my hair and straighten my shirt—it is a little wrinkled. No, Grandma, this time I will go by myself. I don't know why but I feel like walking alone. Don't worry, I am not sad, a long-forgotten emotion is awakening. First I will go to the jewelry store and buy myself a pair of earrings, then perhaps a new dress at the small fabric store. The clear air is so pleasant, I want to meander slowly in the shopping center, casually look at the window shops, examine everything without any hurry. You worry that I will get lost? Why? I know my way here pretty well. Don't worry, Grandma, I am not driven by despair but by a desire to surrender fully to the feminine urge to adorn oneself. The need to beautify is awakened again. Wait for me? No, thank, Grandma, I don't know how long I will be here, and in fact I am not sure I will return to your place later. I was thinking of visiting my apartment, perhaps I will move in there again soon. I thought of the beautiful geranium pots on the small balcony: I forgot to water them, I hope they didn't wither.

Grandma is looking at me, her eyes are glowing; there is no knowing if from pain or joy. She is standing facing me and doesn't know whether to part or to insist on joining me. Out of habit she straightens the hair behind her head. I see she is hesitating whether to say something. To avoid the embarrassment I kiss her on her cheek. Because I am close to her, I smell the scent of perfume blended with a sour odor. She hugs me warmly, coughs a bit, and it seems she has decided to say one more thing. About the job? I don't know, Grandma, I think it is too soon. I promise to consider the offer. I find it hard to imagine myself as a journalist. Yes, I understand you think it has benefits way beyond the professional realm, a path which, even if it is in the public realm, will lead to personal space. But I still can't write.

Grandma is staring at me, her features are softening and her eyes seem enigmatic. She caresses my arm lightly, like a feather touching bare skin. Am I cold? No, I am dressed well. I am on my way now, but I will come to visit you soon. Perhaps I could embrace your way of living even further. I wish I could adopt your past, but it is impossible. Still, I am grateful, Grandma. In your small apartment wide horizons, which I didn't even know existed, were spread out before me. Mom thinks they are useless: without you I would have thought exploring them was a fault, a distortion that should be corrected. Now I want to explore them, even though there may be no turning back.

We leaned one towards the other, head to head, my forehead touching hers, and stood still for a couple of moments. Then I kissed her and left.

The Grammar Teacher

Under my shirt, tucked somewhere between my skirt and my body, I smuggle something out. It may be a camisole I fold to the size of a cigarette pack, perhaps a small piece of tableware I would like to have; a couple of times I have even taken cosmetic creams which I could hardly hide under my arm, they almost fell out as I walked to the exit. First I look to see if the security guards are nearby. If the coast is clear I begin to walk slowly, in a casual manner, towards the exit, making sure to stop on the way to examine another small object so as not to arouse suspicion. About five steps from the door there is always a childish desire to run out, as if it is all a game and I am one step away from winning. In a moment I will cross the store's wide exit doors and the stolen treasure will be mine. But it is here that self-control is needed: a slow and moderate step, one that doesn't betray the wish to escape as quickly as possible.

Sometimes on the way out I have to give up, accept a loss, place the object somewhere and leave empty-handed. The security guards, however, are not inclined to suspect women like me. I often see them following groups of young girls, who hope that if they are caught they will be able to blame each other and the thief won't be arrested. First they gather around the hangers, examining and inspecting, then they decide which garment they want; one of them tucks it into her handbag and together, laughing loudly, they walk slowly and leave the store. The security guards, mostly young and inexperienced men, can't face a group of young women chatting and smiling on their way out. Once, a new guard on his first shift made a mistake and asked the girls where the bathing suit they were holding was. The bursts of laughter and the blunt remarks embarrassed him to tears and he swore he would never stop them again, even if he was absolutely sure they were stealing from the store.

But no one suspects me. I am a woman of somber, respectable appearance. My black hair is simply cut and pulled up in a plain rubber band, my shirts are always tucked in to dark, straight skirts; I carry a gray handbag, I am slightly over-weight but exuding vitality; my entire appearance, aside from my pug nose, speaks of decency and good manners. When I enter the store no one could possibly guess my intentions. Saleswomen treat me kindly, obviously a customer like me must be satisfied; clearly I don't intend to waste my time walking aimlessly between the counters. I pace quickly, as if I were in a hurry to carry out a busy daily routine. There is always a diligent saleswoman who will suggest garments on sale, her instincts leading her to believe I want to make the most of my money. I smile kindly. I am sorry that although she is trying so hard, I refuse politely and keep walking around the store. After she gives up and immerses herself in conversation with other faded and tired saleswomen I advance towards the object I am about to take.

It's been several months now that I have been wandering through stores. I covet things and take them secretly. I never imagined that circumstances would make me do this. I used to think that a person growing up in a stable and respectable family like mine could never end up stealing. I felt I could see my life stretching ahead, and every stage would follow the previous one clearly and naturally. I never imagined I would walk out of a department store with a shirt hidden in my pocket, an overwhelming happiness at not having being caught taking me over completely.

I used to be a grammar teacher. I always knew I would be a teacher. As a child I really liked school; I always answered questions in class and at home correctly, simply, and clearly. The teachers used to comment on my ability to explain everything in a mature and responsible way. I was hard-working and tidy, my books and notebooks were always placed neatly in my backpack; more than once a teacher who lost her notes would ask to take a look at what I had written. In full, rounded handwriting, which never exceeded the top or the bottom of the line, without any decorations or scribbling created by boredom, I wrote down everything that was said in class. I detested children who interrupted. Next to me sat a fat, stupid girl with almond eyes who giggled constantly; if I could have, I would have expelled her from school.

In high school I invested all my energy in learning. My homework was always ready and I never forgot anything at home. Every evening the backpack was placed buckled beside the bed, ready for the next day. My parents were very proud of my achievements, but a couple of times my mother suggested that I spend some time with friends and ease up on the studying. I, however, felt I was standing in a sort of confined zone, whose boundaries must never be crossed. I found it hard to explain, the boys and girls around me seemed to me distant, almost strange, living according to a different inner mechanism, following a tune I never heard. Yet in spite of the isolation from my peers, except for one girl friend, I felt I had a special place in class that couldn't be taken by anyone else.

Of course there were unpleasant moments: next to me sat a slender girl with wide open blue eyes encircled by black paint, ignoring lustful looks and amusing remarks and looking at me with a mixture of wonder and contempt. I would rather have sat alone; the teacher who made her sit next to me said loudly that she was hoping I would encourage her to study more seriously. She merely watched me distantly, wondering what she could possibly learn from me. There were also a couple of boys who used to take my notebooks before class and copy homework, laughing and grabbing the notebook before I agreed that they take it. At first I didn't dare refuse. Later I used to pretend I didn't hear them asking.

But all these embarrassments evaporated when I got the highest grade in class, or when teachers openly praised me. Then I felt everyone acknowledged that my presence in class was worthwhile and justified. Endless hours of studying boiled down to a couple of moments of explicit joy; but they supported me in days in which I was entirely steeped in solving math problems or summarizing history chapters.

Thus, it was only natural that I decided to become a teacher. When I came to my first job interview at a comprehensive school I was excited and somewhat confused. I put on a dark gray skirt and a straight shirt with small buttons, my appearance conveying integrity and earnestness. As I waited behind the closed door of the teachers' room, I saw my reflection in a window—a young woman with a rounded figure, a solemn countenance, squinting in order to detect any invisible flaw that might impede her. Suddenly I saw that a button in my shirt was unfastened; my fingers were shivering as I fastened it, before I was asked to come in. The principal greeted me with a forced smile and asked me to follow him. On the way to his room he ordered the janitor to fix the school's gate, reproached a young teacher for being late for class, and gently rebuked the secretary for not preparing a list of required equipment. When we got to his room he left the door open, and sat down without inviting me to sit. Out of embarrassment I collapsed into one of the chairs, and then he lifted his eyes and looked at me as if seeing me for the first time. He looked at my CV very briefly, as if it was an irksome duty that must be completed, as though I was a student presenting last year's report. Then he asked me about my experience. His expression betrayed neither sympathy nor reservation. Finally, considering every word, he said a teacher was going to leave the school soon, but he was not sure when exactly she would leave or whether a new teacher would be hired to replace her. When she did leave, the school would contact me.

While I was waiting at the bus stop outside the school, a young girl sat next to me, her body soft and adolescent, her face full of acne, carrying a faded, graceless backpack. As the school bell rang, she turned her head backward and looked with hostility at the schoolyard, almost with revulsion. Then she let her hair out of the thin rubber band, twirled it around her short fingers several times and tied it behind her head again, without leaving a single hair to sway in the light wind.

At the next job interview the principal was much nicer. An elderly woman, her face made up not to beautify herself but merely to convey an effort of embellishment. She suggested that I give a grammar class and she would observe my teaching. Of course I consented, but her testing me without letting me know in advance and allowing me to prepare myself made me feel I had failed before I even started. My explanations were vague, I made serious mistakes about issues I knew perfectly well, and towards the end of the class I was confused by a simple question from one of the students. When the bell rang I left the class in a hurry, without even asking the principal if she would consider hiring me.

Finally I got a job at an old, respectable high school with students from well-established families. During the first days I was extremely embarrassed; I felt as if I was a student that was being allowed to substitute for a teacher. In class I shivered a bit, but the students were full of the excitement of the beginning of the school year and didn't notice it. I made several mistakes reading the names, and laughter and gloating erupted in the class. But slowly silence came, the whispers and broken words were hushed, and my voice was heard, stable and clear.

The large, well-lit teachers' room was a hive of activity. The huge windows were wide open and the windowsill packed with textbooks and workbooks. Teachers who hadn't met during the summer break greeted each other loudly, almost shouting. Calls were heard from all corners of the room, a nasty remark about a teacher who had gained weight during the summer, a warm embrace to another teacher who had just gotten married. Some of the male teachers, a small minority among the many women, sat in their armchairs next to the wall and gazed with amusement at their noisy colleagues. A short while before the bell rang the principal entered the room. In spite of his solemn expression, his eyes betrayed a light smile. Due to a stroke half of his face was motionless; as he spoke he filtered the words, orderly and disciplined, never leaving an unfinished sentence or allowing a slang word to creep in. I was told he never engages in idle talk with the teachers, but on the first day of school his face assumes a unique expression resembling a smile, a twitch that could develop into a fully contented countenance and that might even have a touch of humor.

Embarrassed, I looked for a place to sit. At the end of the room, in a shadowy corner, some seats were vacant. I crossed the room cautiously, ignoring the loud voices, and sat on a plain wooden chair beneath the window. The hustle and bustle in the room, the cries, sometimes harsh and graceless, created a sense of disappointment. This is not how I imagined my first day as a teacher; everything about the teachers' room seemed vulgar, lacking the refinement I was expecting to find. Two teachers sat next to me, speaking loudly. The older one was heavily made up, looking more like a sales assistant than a teacher; the younger had short light hair, her dress was plain, almost sloppy, and her strong voice echoed in the room; she burst into roaring laughter and clapped her hands. I sat there, staring at the teachers around me and wondering what went wrong. After a couple of minutes the school secretary came and asked me to fill out some forms. While I was engaged in the details the school bell rang, and all the commotion moved towards the door, fading gradually until all that was heard were thin, quiet voices from the other side of the room and the echoing voices of students playing in the schoolyard.

In the following lessons I managed to establish my straight, moderate voice in the classroom. The students looked at me with a mixture of respect and reservation. The unrestrained bursts of laughter were gone. I outlined the curriculum for the entire year and explained what assignments would be required for each class. I described the exams that would take place during the year. And so the process of studying began, orderly and structured, every class the logical consequence of the previous one. The entire year was spread before them, its limits well set and clearly divided. The distant gaze ahead created a peaceful and pleasant atmosphere in class, which only a couple of moments earlier had been full of a nervous, anxious murmur.

After a few weeks I made friends with a couple of teachers. An elderly lady with a thin, girlish figure and a pointed face used to sit next to me in the teachers' room. She was a biology teacher, constantly complaining about the students: they don't do their homework, they chatter in class, they are indifferent to the material, the boys and girls lack a fundamental curiosity, a desire for knowledge. She makes an effort to prepare the classes, carefully planning every lesson, but all in vain. Her graceless face stretched even further as she became absorbed in this monologue, a long speech with question marks, which she hastily replaced with exclamation marks. In fact, there was no conversation; I sat next to her and she muttered endless complaints. A literature teacher joined us, a woman with a somewhat sad face, who was nearly always checking homework in the teachers' room. She gave endless assignments and read them with a grave expression, as if in one of them the solution to a riddle was concealed. She placed the assignments on the table, a pile of papers, some tidy some wrinkled, written in distorted handwriting, meticulously read them and wrote notes in red ink in the margins—though she had plenty of notes she never exceeded the margins. Finally she placed the papers in a stack, inserted them into a big envelope, and folded the top flap inwards. Then she lifted her brown eyes and looked sadly at the teachers' room, desperate and proud, asking for assurance that she is indeed an extremely devoted teacher.

I also used to check the students' assignments rigorously and fastidiously; I thought homework involved an element of imposing discipline, it was an exercise to tame one's cravings, devoting oneself to a useful but unpleasant activity. Therefore I was very strict when it came to setting assignments. I detested students who didn't prepare their homework; I thought they had a fault that must be corrected, a flaw containing a seed of peril.

After a couple of months everyone knew I was a diligent, committed, and punctilious teacher; true, some said that I was too rigid, I tended to concentrate on every word and to overlook the general context, that perhaps I neglect the personality of the student and ascribe too much importance to test scores. One teacher even suggested that my huge effort conceals a void in my personal life. Had I been married and a mother I wouldn't have spent so much time reading assignments; but all these remarks were insignificant and negligible in comparison to the many compliments I received. The principal, who never joked with the teachers, would pass by me with his twitch that resembled a smile and a nod, and several times he even praised me explicitly. Some teachers openly disapproved of me, as though they considered me a traitor, betraying a common struggle to decrease duties. Others wished to befriend me, sometimes even asking for my advice on assignments and tests.

By the end of the school year everyone acknowledged my special place in school. The brown, faded armchair in the teachers' room was always reserved for me, and even older teachers moved away when I approached it. The students knew I was highly esteemed, and some parents asked to meet me; they would begin by inquiring about their son or daughter but quickly the conversation turned to focus on me, hoping that the affinity between us might prove helpful in future crises. Whenever I entered the classroom the commotion and giggling died down immediately, and I walked at a moderate pace to the teacher's desk. First I would place my books on it, then take out my notebook and turn to the board to write the subject of the day's class.

My gestures in front of the class were slow and confident, I was never hasty. I erased the board with long movements, not stopping to read it but without any hurry; only when the board was completely clean did I begin writing the subject of the lesson in full, rounded letters, distinct but identical in size.

Finally I turned to the students, looking at them gravely, and asked in a low voice who had prepared their homework.

Most of them watched me with awe. Sometimes I felt they could see the pupil that I used to be, a classmate standing in front of them whose sole advantage is that she prepared the material in advance. Yet it was these moments that made me feel my superiority, since even if I had been a student sitting in the first row and writing down every word, I definitely would have been the best in class. Some of them probably would have mocked me, but no one could take away the hint of a smile, subtle but apparent, as I looked around when on my desk there was an A+ exam, marked in red ink.

Once in a while there were unruly students who refused to accept my authority. In one class, a boy sitting next to the window kept staring at the schoolyard throughout the lesson. At first I decided not to say anything though I detested the way he ignored the lesson, like an explicit statement that it would be better to look outside than to pay attention to class. I thought it would be wise to leave him alone. But once in a while he stopped gazing out at the yard, and out of sheer boredom looked at me in a conceited, scornful manner, as if I were the student and he the teacher. I could hardly conceal my embarrassment; I turned immediately to the board, my shoulders rounded and my body shrinking into itself. With broken movements I began writing lengthy lines, so my blushing face could be hidden and the transparent tear would disappear by itself.

Against my better judgment, I was distressed every time I taught this class, as if a latent, obscure danger was materializing, even if momentarily, between the straight wooden chairs and the bright desks, etched with endless diagonal lines. Even before I entered the class I could envisage his beautiful face, decorated with blond curls, green eyes surrounded by almost white eyelashes, always looking into the distance, to the school yard and beyond it. Sometimes he would squint, gazing outwards but looking as if steeped in a dream. Before every class I wavered, considering what I should do; sometimes I was determined to reproach him but I never dared to do so, I was afraid I would look silly: you can't be angry at a student only because he is smiling. Thus I chose to ignore him.

But once, as a girl asked that I repeat an explanation, he burst into loud laughter. His striking beauty prevented others from rebuking him, and the miserable girl sat humiliated and blushing. I heard my voice, loud and harsh, in admonition, speaking of a student's right to get an additional explanation and of the obligation not to embarrass a classmate, but I was horror-stricken. I thought the other students would join in his cheerfulness. In a moment the entire class would be in stitches, the disgraced girl would burst into tears, which would create further joy, more vulgar this time, and my voice would be swallowed in a stream of giggling and cries, the endless gaudy prattle of teenagers.

The handsome boy looked at me with contempt, listening to my reproach and smiling, sitting comfortably in his chair and stretching his legs forward, wondering what his punishment would be. Finally I asked him to leave the class. He sniggered, got up and slowly walked out, as though he had heard that he won a prize and he was going to collect it. When he left the classroom I was relieved. For a moment I feared I had sighed out loud, but as I saw the students returning to their books and notebooks, and the girl still expecting an explanation, I rebuked myself for being so scared: everybody knows I am such a gifted teacher, the fear that my voice won't be heard in class is preposterous, even childish. Only the bell ringing halted the long, fully elaborated and well-reasoned answer to the girl's question.

My parents were very proud of my success. Time and again they inquired how the classes are conducted, whether the students are obedient, what do I teach, how the other teachers like me. In spite of my embarrassment I told them about my success; they sat quietly, absorbing every word, never stopping my fluent speech, but apparently accumulating questions to be asked when I was finished. My father tried to follow the material; he always had remarks that were intended to illustrate how well he knew grammar. My mother was focused on the mundane aspects of school life, her questions always revealing a concern, an anxiety about the future: aren't the other teachers jealous of me? Perhaps they would try to diminish my achievements? She heard of successful people who had failed because of the envy of colleagues. I should be careful not to disagree with senior teachers, try not to emphasize how well I am doing, and prepare everything in advance so no one would complain. So she immersed herself gradually in the troubles that could emerge any moment, struggling with obscure enemies that for her were so real. She lowered her gaze, her voice became somewhat whiny, and it was apparent she could visualize all these dangers that must be avoided; she was about to burst into tears, since in an instant I would be shamefully expelled from school.

Even though I knew every conversation would end this way and that my entire success, which initially had been so pleasant, would metamorphose into a danger that might break out at any time, each time a deep anger was awakened in me, spreading and filling every corner. My mother tried to conceal her anxiety in the recounting of how well I was doing: it was because I was so successful I should be watchful. But I heard the profound doubt in her words, a feeling that my many achievements, which to me seemed so solid, the result of talent and hard work, could disappear in an instant due to dark, obscure forces she failed to understand.

On the last day of the school year a slightly wild spirit prevailed in the teachers' room: cries were heard everywhere, a pile of papers for recycling dropped on the floor and spread all over the room, dirty glasses were left on the tables, and one teacher told a dirty joke out loud. The giggling didn't cease even when the principal entered the room. My two friends seemed alert, as if at the end of the day the invisible tie chaining them to this room—normally subordinated to strict, unequivocal rules but now touched by chaos—would be undone. As the bell heralded the end of the year both teachers and students rushed outside, impatient and nervous, barely stopping themselves from racing to the school doors as they opened with a rasping squeak.

I also stepped outside; already in the corridor, amidst the tumult of the students, among the backpacks rubbing against my arms on their way to the gate, I felt a gloomy spirit overcoming me. I planned to take advantage of the day to do some shopping and pay bills, but as I stood outside the school I felt such a deep distress that I decided to rush home. My bag, normally full of books and assignments, was annoyingly light and insubstantial. I walked away from school, marching briskly to the bus stop; all of a sudden I decided to return. I reproached myself for escaping from school, for joining the run to the gate without making sure that my stuff was safely locked away. I turned back and entered the building, which was by now completely empty except for faint voices coming from the upper floor. I walked slowly along the corridor towards the teachers' room, finding it hard to accept the silence. An annoying thought crossed my mind: now the school resembles a market without any merchants; the food stands are untouched, full and seductive, but customers and vendors are all gone. I entered the teachers' room and went to my locker. But next to the locker I saw a small wrinkled piece of paper on the floor, torn from a full page, written in a rounded handwriting. I picked it up and read: *I thought about what you said and have reached the conclusion that you were right, there is no knowing what she will do, you had better watch out...*

I dropped the paper, tossed my books into my bag, and ran in panic to the entrance; once again I saw the familiar pictures on the wall, the sports trophies, and the announcement of an end-of–the-year party, but I ran, gasping and breathless, in order to exit the school gate as quickly as possible.

During the summer I met Matan, my future husband. He introduced himself: a computer engineer in a developing company. He looked like a hard-working, ambitious man, determined to invest most of his time and talent in his job. When I saw him for the first time I could hardly conceal a smile. He had on a ribbed shirt, ironed and tight, tucked into pants with a laundry scent. When the shirt became slightly stained by the ice cream we were eating, he looked at me deeply embarrassed, as if he had failed to conceal a shameful flaw. Immediately he asked where I worked, and when I told him I was a teacher I saw content in his eyes, though he tried to disguise it. He asked me why I chose this profession. My explanations, about a desire to educate young people, to teach them the right habits, were loose, almost misleading. Finally I simply admitted that it was a natural choice, I had never considered any other occupation; my childhood and adolescent experience had made me become a teacher. Even though I saw he was relaxed and feeling at ease, I kept describing how well I was doing and added that in the coming years I might attempt to be appointed head grammar teacher in school.

Our wedding was attended not only by the principal and several teachers but also by the heads of the computer company employing Matan. The president, a chubby old man with hair dyed black, kissed me gracefully. He embraced Matan, and as he was holding him in his curved arm he turned to me and said in a pleasant, cordial manner that I should remember that we are family, and that from now on I am part of it too, and added that I should feel free to approach him with any problem or concern at any time. In the confusion of the wedding I didn't pay attention to these words; but in the following days I was often bewildered by what he had said, inviting and uninhibited, moving me from the office to the warm bosom of the family, as if the gap between superior and subordinates didn't exist. When I told my mother about it she looked at me, distant and absorbed in thoughts, and then asked me how long Matan had been working in this company. My father, overhearing the conversation from the next room, burst angrily into the kitchen. He was proud of Matan and thought he was a gifted, successful husband, and in no way was he willing to accept any doubt regarding the future flourishing career of his son-in-law. He reproached my mother and said he didn't understand why she has to doubt everything; apparently the president really felt that Matan and I are part of the company's family, and no wedding greeting could have been more appropriate and touching.

At the end of the summer I returned to school. I found the hubbub of the students pleasant, I walked along the corridors, pretending to look for someone just so I could listen to the calls and giggles, to smell the odor of teenagers, and to see how they walked into class with joy and not with desperation.

As always, the first class was devoted to a description of the curriculum for the entire year. I wrote on the board the subjects that would be taught, how many classes would be devoted to each subject, and what the required assignments would be. I was careful to explain the value of homework, how an extra revision of the material deepens our knowledge and, most of all, that learning habits are the foundation on which human knowledge is constructed. To create a certain connection with the students I admitted that youngsters of their age are normally preoccupied with things other than homework—words that generated pleasant smiles in the classroom—but still they must understand that discipline is a vital instrument for success in any field, and only a constant and structured effort would lead to achievements. This is the reason, I added, that I ascribe so much importance to homework and why in each class I would check if they were prepared properly.

My lessons were conducted in perfect order; the classes were quiet, with a touch of tension. The material was presented in a clear and simple way; therefore the students understood it very well. In exams at the school, my classes always got the highest scores for each grade. The principal pointed this out in the teachers' monthly journal, and added his congratulations. My two friends were somewhat surprised, though everyone knew I was an esteemed teacher. The biology teacher, her face gloomy, said that apparently the students were more interested in grammar than in biology, and no wonder, they would use it in real life whereas biology would remain nothing more than a part of their general knowledge. The literature teacher looked at me sadly, trying to compliment me, but her gaze betrayed an inarticulate complaint.

My excellent reputation made students who refused to study look unruly or lazy. Some were angry at my fastidiousness, at the way I emphasized that assignments must be fully completed. In one class I encountered a slim girl with honey-colored hair almost down to her waist, who never prepared her homework. Whenever I reprimanded her she said nothing, blushing and looking at me with a penetrating look, full of wonder, as if she couldn't understand why I insisted on creating such obstacles. Since her manner lacked any impertinence or insolence, I found it hard to enforce my way. Whatever I did was in vain: every time she was asked, she blushed and answered she hadn't prepared her homework.

I don't know why, I simply couldn't accept the way she ignored any threat or punishment, acting as if school was a remote hotel she happened to be visiting where for some strange reason the manager of the hotel insisted that she clean her room. I decided to talk to her in private, without her classmates watching her in anticipation, alert to see how she would answer my question. As we entered a side room at school, she seemed embarrassed and shy. She stood motionless and waited for me to sit down, her face flushed but looking at me with concentration. I began by saying I don't want to hurt her, on the contrary, I like her very much and I see she is an intelligent, talented girl, but she won't meet the school's requirement if she doesn't practice at home. I added an explanation of the importance of constant perseverance, a striving not limited to a single achievement, brilliant as it might be, but to continuous progress, which is the only way to achieve anything substantial.

She looked at me with her huge eyes, making no attempt to refute my arguments or answer me. For a moment I thought she didn't hear me, but immediately I reproached myself, this is a silly thought, clearly she is listening but she doesn't respond. After minutes of explanations, which seemed extremely long due to her continuing silence, I decided to demand an explanation of her.

If the meeting had taken place today I think I would have burst into tears; perhaps I would even have embraced her and kissed her cheek when I heard her answer; but at that time she provoked a latent anger, a fury I didn't know existed within me. Very simply, without any pretense, she said there is no need for that since once she graduated from high school she intended to move to a secluded village in the Galilee and live a plain, rural life, devoid of any professional ambition, and her most ardent wish was to sit on the porch and watch the view, especially during the evening hours, since the light is so soft and pleasant then.

When I answered her I realized my back was arched and my hands were joined fiercely. My voice sounded metallic, I used pompous language, words I would normally avoid. I spoke about duties everyone has, man's responsibility to his society, I even said something about the moral implications of our actions. Though I knew I was using vague, empty clichés, I had no intention of stopping. Anger filled me, like a strange bubbling, as if my inner organs were disarranged and the order within my body was being violated; the wrath wasn't directed outwards but it was merely pushing every organ away. Finally I was silent, and she looked at me with eyes full of wisdom, as if she was sharing my pain due to a misfortune or loss. Then I added that if she didn't change her habits she wouldn't be permitted to participate in the class, and at the end of the year she wouldn't be allowed to continue to the next grade. She looked at me surprised, her face reddening and in her eyes a film of tears. In spite of the harsh threat she tried to understand the source of my arbitrary decision, but I added nothing and left.

One Saturday we dined at my parents' place. The table was covered with an embroidered tablecloth with a delicate flower print. My mother decided to use the beautiful porcelain dishes, reserved for festive dinners. Next to every plate was a matching napkin, and beautiful glasses, long and oval, stood at a perfect distance from the plates. All the lights were on, reflected in the large glass bowls at the center of the table, and the room, that normally looked ordinary and even sloppy, was now dignified and inviting.

My father questioned Matan about his work. He never got tired of listening to stories about the computer company. He remembered every piece of gossip about junior employees and memorized any information on the senior staff. Matan began telling my father about a quarrel that had taken place at the office: the manager was angry at a young engineer who was negligent in his work and went home early in the evening, leaving on his desk e-mails that should have been answered instantly. The young engineer pulled his long hair behind his head, removed his glasses and put them on the desk, and replied that though he cares dearly about his work he refuses to be enslaved by it, and even if he doesn't complete all the tasks by the end of the day, he will hurry home to be with his children.

Matan and my father disapproved of the insolent reply of the young engineer; my father noted, smiling, that perhaps he is not that smart, and Matan replied with a blink of agreement. My father said that you can't just leave everything and walk away at five o'clock; one has a responsibility to the company, which may lose valuable contracts if the engineers don't stay on schedule. Matan added that in order to work at a computer company and to achieve certain goals, one has to be consistent over time.

Everyone thinks that computer guys succeed due to one brilliant idea, but the truth is that success is the result of constant hard work, and sometimes it takes years to execute an idea that was born almost randomly, in an idle conversation.

To support his point I told them about the student who never prepares homework and my conversation with her. As I concluded, I saw my mother putting down the boiling soup pot on the table, and staring at me. She seemed surprised, perhaps by my determined arguments, or maybe by my explicit threats; but her gaze revealed no satisfaction. Her thick eyebrows curved, she looked down at the table and began pouring soup into the small bowls. Matan and my father, unlike her, listened carefully to the details of the story, and as I concluded they began speculating on the student—maybe she quarrels with her parents, maybe it is an unstable family, perhaps her parents are uneducated and don't know she is not preparing homework, perhaps she lies to them. I was forced to admit I don't know anything about her family, but obviously she can't go on like this, it's clear, she understands it very well.

My mother seemed very disturbed by my story. In a low voice, as if a stranger was speaking from within her, she asked whether it was possible that the girl was telling the truth, that she indeed intends to move to a farm in the Galilee and therefore she is indifferent to success at school. Matan only smiled slightly, suffocating a giggle out of politeness, and after a couple of moments asked if he could have some more of my mother's wonderful chicken which today, as always, was juicy and tasty. She gave him some more chicken, adding baked potatoes, and smiled at him aloofly, in her eyes a touch of ridicule, not to say contempt.

As we left, Matan hugged me warmly and complimented the way I had spoken with the student. He apologized—he didn't want to say it in front of my mother, but sometimes she doesn't understand what it is all about. He, however, is very proud of me, he wishes all the teachers would act like me. Gently he ran his hand through my hair, carefully, as if he had just found out how precious I was, and now there was a double need to take care of me.

Towards the end of the year national assessment tests to evaluate the students' achievements took place. A gloomy spirit took over the school. The teachers were inclined to speak less in the teachers' room, as if every moment should be devoted to preparing for the exams. In the many teachers' meetings that took place in the evening hours, various suggestions were raised as to how to improve the scores. At first everyone sat next to a clean, tidy table, with plates full of cakes, juice bottles standing in two rows at its ends. But during the meeting, often prolonged into the night, pieces of cake dropped on the table, spreading crumbs which mixed with the sheets of paper scattered all around; disposable plastic cups fell on their side, rolling on their stomachs as the last drops of juice dripped on the table. The colorful napkins that the secretary bought were scattered all around, wrinkled and torn, hiding food residue in their folds, and some even fell to the floor and were left there untouched. The bottles passed from hand to hand, one accidently slipped on the table and left a golden puddle, which dripped to the floor. The secretary rushed to clean the syrupy fluid, but annoyingly it refused to be absorbed by the damp mop, and drops were smeared all over the table, leaving a trail of napkins dipped in sweet, sticky juice.

I sat there self-absorbed, holding my cup. My skirt remained straight and tight, free of crumbs. I never said a word, the agitation around the table was strange to me; I knew with full certainty that my students' scores would be excellent. Months of organized, structured work would no doubt bear worthy fruits.

When the results of the tests were posted I smiled shyly. On the bulletin board in the teachers' room they were arranged according to class and teacher. As I saw the papers hanging on the board I was a bit anxious, but a quick glance revealed that the scores of my classes were extremely high, and in one class they were even the highest in the country. A couple of teachers complimented me, but I smiled and looked down modestly, my countenance conveying humility. As the bell rang, I walked slowly to the classroom.

A couple of minutes after the beginning of the class a knock was heard at the door, and immediately it opened with a squeak. At the entrance stood the principal, and next to him was a woman of about my age, dressed very elegantly, her face made up and her light straight hair well-coiffed. As they entered the room the principal gestured that I should continue with my work. They stood in the corner, next to the wall, whispering and looking at me and at the students. The principal smiled at her; it was like a twitch of pain. There was something strange in his expression, a hint of a weakness he had never exposed. The woman moved her head in agreement, her hair moving forward and backward, and then, in a casual manner, she stretched one foot forward and leaned it on the thin, high heel of a red, shining sandal.

During class I wondered who she might be; probably a supervisor from the Ministry of Education who had come to watch a lesson due to the high scores of this class in the national assessments. Then I thought she might be a member of one of the many delegations that often visited the school. Dressed in an elegant shirt tucked in a straight, flattering skirt, her hair perfectly styled, by her appearance it was evident she was not a member of the staff. As I was asking the students questions and they replied, she laughed quietly with the principal, and then they both turned and left the class. I don't know why, but I felt angry. Normally I was indifferent to visitors in the classroom, I perceived them as a necessity that couldn't be avoided. But something about the posture of this woman, her cold look, the foot in the red shining sandal that she stretched gracefully forward, made me seethe with rage. As the bell rang I quickly collected my stuff and hastened to the teachers' room, wishing to tell my friends about the annoying visit.

But as I entered the room I ran into the principal and the visitor. With a straight face he signaled me to come, and as I approached them he introduced her: a new grammar teacher, she came from a very prestigious school, and now we were extremely fortunate, so he said, that she had agreed to be part of our school. The teacher shook my hand coldly, examining me with a disengaged curiosity, while I stood before her discomforted and shy, wondering why the school needed another grammar teacher. The principal added that we should meet and discuss the teaching materials, looking at me indifferently and then smiling at her. She nodded, her hair bouncing back and forth, thanked him abruptly, and without waiting for his response turned around and left the teachers' room. The principal's gaze followed her and as she exited the room he muttered something about how we should decide together about the requirements, and then gave another vague sentence regarding fruitful cooperation between the two of us; his black eyes were wide open but he seemed like a blind man watching shadows and trying to make sense of them.

As I dropped into the armchair in the corner of the room I heard the word 'cooperation' over and over again. A dark, gloomy cloud began to take form in my mind, something somber and turbid; I felt other teachers were talking to me from behind a screen, as if they were far away, though they could reach out and touch me. I tried to convince myself that the somber spirit was created by mistake, by confusion, by a misunderstanding that would be resolved soon. Maybe the principal hadn't seen the test scores: surely when he saw them everything would change, return to its normal course, and there would be no need for a new grammar teacher. But beneath this dismal spirit I could see the red, shiny sandals, the tight flattering skirt with a slit on the right side, the hair bobbing from side to side, and the eyes staring aloofly at the principal and me.

When I told my mother about all this she shook her head in desperation. I waited for the right moment, and only when the two of us were alone in the kitchen did I tell her about the new teacher, so that my father and Matan wouldn't hear about it. She followed every word, took interest in every detail, like someone who had predicted a terrible disaster and now wants to find out how exactly it came to be. I tried to describe the new teacher, but the details seemed insignificant, irrelevant. No, she is not exceptionally beautiful, though she is very feminine, but something about her appearance is too erect and stiff. I am positive there isn't a trace of hubbub in her class: I suppose she intimidates the students with her low, quiet voice, without saying anything explicitly dominating. When Matan and my father entered the kitchen we became silent. They felt a conversation was interrupted and tried to inquire what it was about, but my mother looked down and began washing the dishes, while I left the kitchen immediately.

At the beginning of the week, as I entered the classroom and placed my books on the desk, the door opened and the principal and the new teacher appeared once again. Wearing a tight dress with a floral print design and the red sandals, she smiled at the students, and stood right next to me. I was horror-struck; the notebook I was holding dropped to the floor, the pen rolled on the desk and stopped at the very corner, right before falling down. I bent to pick up the notebook but in my confusion bumped my head into the corner of the desk. I felt my face flushing, my hands shivering slightly, and for a moment I thought I would burst into tears. But then I told myself I was behaving like a silly child, surely there is a perfectly acceptable explanation for her standing next to me, in a moment the humiliation will turn out to be a mistake, an error that will be rectified immediately.

But the principal looked indifferently at me with a straight face, a vibrating chin and quiet, practical eyes—he stood before the class, waiting for silence. He began by saying that a new grammar teacher was coming to our school, a talented, successful teacher whom we are fortunate to have with us, and she will teach this lesson instead of the permanent teacher. He didn't say my name, only called me the 'permanent teacher'. He was asking the students to behave well and assist the new teacher to become part of our school. After these short sentences he left the class in haste.

A girl sitting in the first row is watching me with pity. I freeze, I don't know if I should step aside and leave or stay and watch her teach. My expression may resemble a smile, but my body is motionless and disobeys me, refusing to go away, yet unable to claim its place. As I am stretching a hesitant hand and leaning on the desk, the new teacher steps forward then stands facing the first row of desks. Her body is peaceful and tall, she doesn't straighten her shirt or push a lock of hair to its place, but turns to the students and in a low, quiet voice she says that in this lesson we will talk about a new subject that hasn't been taught so far, the analysis of complex sentences. For a single moment I become the student I used to be. I want to raise my hand and say that this subject is not a part of this year's curriculum; immediately I understand how pointless and futile these words would be. In small, hesitant steps, looking neither at the students nor at the new teacher, I walk toward the door and exit the class.

I walked through the corridors as if I were blind, oblivious of where the walls are and whether I should turn left or right. A student who passed by said something, but I heard nothing but noise. I reached the teachers' room, drew my handbag out of the small locker, opened it and looked for my purse and the keys, though no one had ever touched them, and when I found them I closed the locker, took my handbag and walked in a strange, disjointed way out of the school, without letting anyone know that I was leaving or asking someone to substitute for me in the next classes. After a strained walk of about half an hour, I found myself at the entrance to my parents' home.

My mother, who opened the door, looked at me in silence and made an inviting gesture with her hand. Even before I told her what had happened tears began running down my cheeks, and she wiped them quickly with a folded tissue. The principal, the new teacher, the red sandals, the notebook that fell down and the way my head had bumped into the desk, they all accumulated to form a pile of discontents, yet their order was unclear and it was impossible to tell which one preceded the other; eventually they amalgamated into a future disaster from which there could be no escape.

My mother listened to me mutely, asking nothing, only nodding as if she was familiar with the story but wanted to make sure that I was recounting it correctly and that the details were accurate. Finally I was silent, and she kept shaking her head from one side to the other, like a person who knows a calamity is looming and cannot be avoided. So we sat together in silence. She kept nodding her head and making a small sigh once in a while and I stared at the embroidered tablecloth, my tears dried and my face red and swollen. Finally she said that maybe I would be able to find a job as a grammar teacher in another school.

A terrible rage took over me, an anger that spread and became physically painful. I felt as if an animal was running in panic within my body, unable to find its way out. I almost grabbed the vase from the table and tossed it against the wall. Again I pictured the new teacher and the principal, and then I looked at my mother: she should have cried out, come to my defense, struggled with the new teacher, and instead she lowered her gaze, yielding, suggesting that I escape before the iron school gate would slam behind me. All the good manners are gone, a daughter's respect for her mother, it's all over. I began shouting, accusing her of encouraging me to give up and not to struggle, she should have been there for me, who knows, maybe she even thinks the new teacher is really better than me. I stood there screaming, making ridiculous, preposterous accusations, arguing that she never appreciated me, complaining she thinks Matan is more gifted than I am, reminding her how my father knows the names of every employee at Matan's workplace but he never asked what the teachers are called; finally I even said that perhaps she prefers that I fail, it would be easier this way. She sat there looking at me, neither replying nor denying, in her eyes a new, unfamiliar tinge of despair. As I turned to the door it crossed my mind that I had never noticed that she is a bit hump-backed. I pushed the thought away and left my parents' place, slamming the door behind me, ignoring the welcome of a neighbor, and bursting into the street, full of red sunshine.

I don't know how long I walked. I saw nothing but dusty pavements, the white stripes of zebra crossings, feet in shoes walking next to me. Every now and then I bypassed pits and other obstacles, once I almost slipped and fell but I grabbed an iron rail and kept walking. In one alley an old woman with a dark scarf on her head said something to me, but I didn't understand her; I nodded and kept walking. Only when I felt exhausted and couldn't walk anymore did I realize I was not far from my own place. After a couple of minutes I climbed up the stairs and drew out the keys; then the door opened and Matan stretched his arms towards me and embraced me.

First I cried, the teacher, the principal, the desk, the sandals, they were all transformed into one, long whine. My nose running, my hair disheveled, my eyes full with tears, I told him everything. Matan again embraced me warmly, wiped my tears with his fingers and said we must calculate our next steps. When I went into the kitchen I saw a fresh salad in a nice bowl, sweet-smelling, freshly baked bread, various cheeses: he had prepared dinner for the both of us. Moved and excited I sat down, and he put food in my plate.

While I began to eat he was thinking out loud. My mother had called him and told him what happened today. He simply couldn't figure out why the principal wants to hire a new teacher, I have such an excellent record, one only has to take a brief look at the national test scores to see it. And why this teacher in particular? Is he acquainted with her? Perhaps they worked together somewhere, perhaps there is even a romantic issue here. My mother said she is too elegant, and completely unafraid of him—in fact it is the other way around, it seems that he is the one who is scared of her. Matan kept talking, determined to reach an accurate description of the teacher though he had never seen her, but I felt his depiction of the unfolding of events had a hidden purpose. He emphasized again and again the tight dress, the somewhat vulgar sandals, the brash, or at least extroverted, character, her apparent vanity, and even the complete silence in the class as she stood strong and erect facing the students. Finally, in a casual manner, he added that perhaps it would be wise of me to adopt some of these habits: clearly they would very useful to my career, and it could be argued that they are much more important than diligence and a continuous structured effort.

The walls of the kitchen turned vague, the delicate flowers on the tablecloth became blurred and the food residue on the plate blended into an obscure stain. I tried to comprehend Matan's arguments but fatigue overtook me. For a moment I felt as if the entire kitchen was moving slowly. Matan saw my expression and said that perhaps I was not feeling well, I had such a hard day, I had walked for several hours, I had better lie down. He held my hand and I got up, went after him and relaxed on the bed. He took off my clothes, overcoming the obstacle of opening a button or a zipper as if it was a major task, and then he began to fondle me.

I am exhausted and Matan is absorbed in my curves, his hand seems heavy, and now I realize that he is crossing the boundaries, granting himself a new freedom, daring to touch me as if I were a stranger, as if we met in this room by chance and in a moment each one of us will go his own way. At first I try to protest, but weakness and pleasure prevent me from resisting him, and so we are caught in a whirlpool, both overpowering and illusive.

The next morning I decided to approach the principal directly. There was no point in being cautious, soon the new teacher would take my place. I put on a tight, straight skirt, tucked into it an ironed shirt; my face portrayed courage and even a hint of humor. When I got to school I turned immediately to the principal's office. The secretary greeted me kindly. In a deep, husky voice she said hello and then asked how she could help me. She is very sorry, the principal is busy today, important appointments from early morning until late evening, could I tell her what it is about? No, of course, she understands. *By the way, did you have a chance to meet the new grammar teacher? Amazing woman, isn't she? So elegant, so talented, they say that as she enters the classroom the students are simply eager to study. We are so fortunate that she accepted the job offer at our school, it is teachers like her that make this school such a prestigious institution.* In a moment she will ask the principal when he can meet me.

She stretched a rough hand, full of rings and with long red fingernails, to the phone and pushed an invisible button, whispering into the receiver and watching me; then she said in her hoarse voice that the principal hopes he will have time tomorrow. She will look for me at the teachers' room and let me know when I can meet with him. As she saw the disappointment on my face she faked a smile, and promised that the appointment would indeed take place. I stood there in front of her embarrassed, as if I was a student reporting late for class, trying to convince the secretary that it wasn't my fault, that circumstances beyond my control made me linger elsewhere. Before I left I said again that the appointment is very important for me, and she smiled and assured me that she would let me know as soon as possible when I could meet with the principal.

As I entered the class where the new teacher had replaced me I felt a certain laxity, as if a hidden, invisible stitch had been unraveled. The students didn't hasten to sit down, a couple of boys kept talking even though I sat in my place, a kind of murmur was heard in the classroom, half-words, whispers, and a quiet giggling, even a long cough, which normally would stop abruptly as the teacher enters the class. As I got up the whispers decreased, but a buzz kept rolling through the class, vague and soft. When I turned to the board and began writing the subject of the lesson I heard behind me, loud and clear, laughter expanding in the classroom.

Already then, as I stood with my back to the students, I knew something had gone wrong and couldn't be fixed; in an instant it hit me that all this gradual, constructed effort was in vain, a futile attempt to advance to a place no one wanted to reach. For a moment I saw the image of my mother, sad and modest, and immediately she disappeared and I heard the roaring, derisive laughter again. I should have ignored the noise coming from the class but habit made me turn around to the students.

Two boys sitting at the far end of the classroom next to the wall were laughing out loud, grabbing the desk and chair in a twitch, as if the laughter had been imposed on them. The other students looked at them and at me alternately, wondering what would happen now. In a loud, harsh voice I asked what was so funny. Something about my tone made one of them stop roaring. With a face full with tears he sputtered that his friend had told him a joke. Had he apologized, muttered something about being sorry, I would have gone on with class. But his provocative words, the amused voice, and the insinuating looks at his friend still choking with laughter made me furious; it was a rage I often saw in other teachers but I was inclined to dismiss it, to perceive it as evidence of weakness, perhaps even of laziness.

A cry startled the classroom. As I heard my voice it crossed my mind that it resembled a saw cutting rusty iron. *Get out*, I screamed, *get out and don't come back, there is no room for students like you in my class.* The laughing boys were silent: apparently they had never suspected the quiet, polite teacher could shout like that. They both stood motionless, paralyzed by surprise, looking at me and wondering whether I might burst into laughter and all this would turn out to be a silly joke. The eyes of one of the boys were filled with tears, in a minute he would be crying; he leaned on the desk as if he was about to fall down, reclining his head and looking down at the floor, attempting to conceal the tears that began rolling slowly on the smooth cheek. Then his friend looked at him and said quietly: *if he goes, so do I.*

In a gesture of resolve I raised my hand and pointed at the door. I stood motionless, without dropping the hand, as the two of them stepped outside: both thin, one short and sloppy, the other with a slightly bent back. Only as the door was shut did I drop my hand and turn to the board. Even though I asked a couple of questions, no one replied. The silence oppressing the room was so heavy that even when the bell rang the students remained seated, while adolescent voices and brisk foot-tapping were heard from the corridor.

I collected my things and walked slowly to the teachers' room. As I entered, my friend hurried towards me, grabbing my hand and pulling me as if someone was chasing us and we needed to escape.

I heard what happened in class, she whispered in my ear, *these students are obnoxious; they should be expelled from school, so disrespectful, they think they can do anything, shameless, everyone is talking about it, they came crying to the teachers' room and talked with one of the teachers, and she called the principal, and he spoke with them at length. Perhaps their parents will be called to school, I hope this time they will learn a lesson.*

As I followed her, slowly other teachers began asking me what happened in class, with obvious excitement. I tried to explain— the mocking laughter, the twitching, the degrading words about a joke, but it all sounded so foolish now, lacking the insolence of the roaring laughter, almost like a childish prick, something that would evoke, at most, a warning look.

As the teachers were surrounding me, repeating my words and interpreting every gesture, the secretary came in. Now she wasn't smiling anymore; though her face was heavily made up and pink, clown-like circles were drawn on her two cheeks, her expression was as grave as could be. In her low, husky voice she muttered that the principal would see me the next day at ten o'clock, dropped a pile of papers on the table and left.

As the teachers around me were contemplating what I should say to the principal, one suggesting that I demand that the students be expelled, another saying they should be forgiven, I saw at the far end of the room the new teacher, sitting in the armchair, alert and probing and following the excitement around me. She sat erect, her bare legs crossed, wearing a dark dress and a golden necklace, her light hair swinging with the movement of the head, and her eyes watching me with a mixture of curiosity and contempt. I closed my eyes for a moment; then I tossed my books and notebooks into my handbag, said goodbye to the teachers and left school almost in a run.

Sky frightfully bright, sunlight nauseatingly blinding, wind carrying dust from a remote desert; I walked slowly, dragging my feet aimlessly only to be able to endure the distress spreading within me, threatening to become a huge growth that might suffocate me. One step after the other, the tears pouring down my face, my entire body struggling not to fall down and collapse.

I hear the cellphone ringing in my purse but I don't answer. The streets of the city change, first I walk in broad avenues under the wide leafs of palm trees, then the streets fill with small fabric stores, furniture and house decoration shops, and finally I think I am in poorer quarters. My feet ache, I hurry to a bench in a small park and relax onto it as if it was a comfortable armchair. Then I realize the cellphone keeps ringing. Matan is looking for me. Someone called from school and said I didn't attend class, they don't know where I am. He is very busy with work now but distracted by his concern. Am I out of my mind, to disappear like that? Where am I? He will come to pick me up immediately. I don't know in what street? What is wrong with me? Here, the name of the street is written. I will sit still, I won't move from the bench; he will be there in a couple of minutes.

When we got home I lay motionless on the black sofa. Matan kept asking what had happened in school; though I did try, I was unable to tell him anything. The words didn't add up to full sentences, the grammar was faulty, instead of saying 'school' I kept saying 'synagogue', and when trying to depict the secretary threatening me with an appointment with the principal tomorrow, I had to repeat the description several times since it was impossible to tell whether she had approached me or I was the one who asked for the appointment. I wanted to describe the teachers surrounding me and the new teacher gazing arrogantly at me from a distance, but all I could say was that I have no more strength, I can't fend off the people around me anymore, and that I am tired to death.

I woke up after two hours. As I opened my eyes I knew a vague danger was slowly materializing but I couldn't remember what it was. The anguish remained, as oppressive as ever, but lacking a distinct shape. Something ceased to be what it was, it was broken and could never be mended, but what was it? Murmuring voices emerged from the kitchen; I heard my parents and Matan whispering. Only when I heard them repeat the word *Principal* did I recall everything. The events of the day unfolded in my mind, the wild laughter, the weeping students, the teachers whose tranquility had been disturbed, and the secretary threatening me that tomorrow morning the principal would see me.

I got up from bed and walked to the kitchen. My parents and Matan sat around the table. As I entered they seated me on a chair as if I was sick, and my mother placed a cup of tea in front of me. They stood around me, their faces revealing concern and devotion, watching me and wondering how to start a conversation. Finally my father cleared his throat, caressed me lightly, and said he had heard that something happened again in school, apparently it was very serious, otherwise it would be inconceivable that I should leave school without saying a word, and it was practically impossible that I forgot a class was scheduled. Something about his tone made me feel resentful, he spoke to me as if I was a naughty child: you don't want to shout at her but she shouldn't be allowed to carry on with her tricks, she should be addressed softly but told very clearly that order and discipline must be kept. But in spite of the anger I managed to tell them, slowly and in sequence, all that had happened that day in school. When I was done they remained silent, immersed in their thoughts.

My father sat next to me, running his bony hands through his hair out of habit; he was wearing a ribbed shirt with brown and blue stripes, faded and old-fashioned, with a detergent odor. I saw he wasn't sure what he should say. Finally, in his deep voice, he said that sometimes people don't understand properly what is going on at the workplace, and this is particularly true for those growing up in a warm, supportive environment, among loving family members; they are unfamiliar with a strict approach and they tend to interpret any blunt word as an insult. However, I have to understand—now he was looking at me directly—the students are indeed rude but it is impossible to walk away during school hours. In spite of the vulgarity, the lack of discipline, the teacher should set an example for the others. He understands my agitation but I was wrong. He is positive that this is exactly what the principal will say when I see him tomorrow.

My mother looked at him. For a moment a hint of a smile appeared on her sad face and then it evaporated. She sat next to me and caressed me, her hand touching my hair, my face, my arm. It was her silence, fondling me but saying nothing, that brought me to tears. It's all lost, this is what she is thinking, the new teacher will take my place and there is no way to reverse the verdict. Nothing can beat the tall, erect posture, the arrogant look, the hair swinging forward and backward with the movement of the head, the red sandals, not even absolute success in the national tests. I had better leave as soon as possible, before being expelled shamefully.

Matan said nothing. But in the evening, when we were alone at home, he began explaining what should be done, speaking rapidly, without breathing between the sentences, every observation creating a new concern. It would be wise to meet with the principal but it might make things worse, if I don't present my achievements maybe the principal won't take them into account, but clearly he is aware of the test scores, but if he knows, why did he hire the new teacher? She may be a good teacher, and clearly her appearance is an advantage, but doesn't the principal want his school to do well in the national tests? Obviously he does, so how can he even consider replacing me with another teacher? The thread of thought was tangled, twisted and curved, sometimes disappearing and then emerging at an unexpected place, becoming a dense, matted skein, a knot that couldn't be unsnarled, and all of Matan's attempts to grab an end of the thread and untie it were bitter and insulting.

Late at night Matan hugs me, kisses my forehead, and fondles my hair. His face reveals his pain. He creases his eyebrows; I can feel his disturbed look even though his eyes are closed. I also shut my eyes, lying covered and motionless in bed, and then I feel his hand, crossing the limits again, dominating me, perhaps even with a touch of aggression. I open my eyes and look at him. Strange, but there is a sparkle of joy in his eyes, a glimpse of victory, sorrow mixed with provocation. He is not afraid that I will refuse, that I will avoid his body, acting as if he can do with me whatever he wishes, careful not to hurt me but fully absorbed by his pleasure. *Enough, Matan*, I push him away, *leave me alone.* He is looking at me with surprise, as if he has just found out that I am there, withdrawing slowly, turning his back to me, and after a couple of minutes I hear a slow, steady breathing.

The next morning I pushed the closet doors wide open and examined the dresses: one was white with tiny flowers scattered on it, a light summer dress that I had bought in a moment of weakness a day after I met Matan. Another one was brown with a narrow cut, I purchased it for a friend's wedding but it was left untouched in the closet. There was also a blue dress with buttons, not too light and not too elegant; it glided easily onto my body. The high-heeled pumps were painful, my feet felt contorted, as though in a splint, but I paced slowly to the mirror and put mauve lipstick on my lips.

When Matan saw me he was speechless. His eyes were wide open, I couldn't tell if it was lust or disgust. His expression, like that of a boy watching a magic show who can't believe what he sees, made me smile. Then he got a grip on himself and muttered: *are you out of your mind?*

At exactly ten o'clock I got to school and turned to the principal's office. The secretary examined me head to toe, faking a smiling without concealing her contempt, and then she said in her deep husky voice that the principal is still busy; please be seated in the waiting hall, she will call me when he is available. After a couple of minutes she pointed her colored finger, suggesting I should enter his office. The principal was immersed in writing. Without diverting his look, he mumbled between his teeth *sit down*.

I sat on a brown armchair, my heart pounding and I hardly breathed, repeating to myself the speech I had prepared at home: I would open with an apology, perhaps hint that I wasn't feeling well, and then immediately elaborate on my various achievements, without modesty, and refer in detail to the national tests scores. I had better not say anything about the new teacher, it would make me look petty, I should focus on my own advantages. This speech, which I memorized carefully all the way to school, now turned nebulous, parts of it disappeared. I couldn't extricate them, and the words were stored in my memory without any logical sequence. But as I was trying to reconstruct it, to gather the various parts into a whole, the principal raised his eyes and looked at me.

A horrible smile, mean and mocking, spread in an instant across his face. Even though his big dark eyes remained frigid under his black thick eyebrows, a wide smile emerged on half of his face, revealing perfectly straight and identical teeth, almost as if they were machine-made; the other side of the mouth was inclined downwards. A scornful snort followed this twitch, like an engine's blowing, a roaring that had it not immediately followed a smile one would have thought revealed resentment, or even anger. Exactly as the smile appeared in an instant, so it died in a split second, disappearing without a trace. Only the dark eyes watched me with concentration, and an irksome silence spread through the room.

I felt my back wet, my fingers were stuck on the sides of the armchair and my feet were painfully deformed in my pumps. I thought I heard bells ringing, something like a whistle, a rising and descending voice, like a screen with a low voice emerging from behind it, *you can't walk away whenever you feel like it, you have a responsibility to the students, what kind of example are you setting, any one of them might think that he or she can skip school whenever they feel like it, if a student behaved this way she would be severely punished, and now I will have to consider what to do.* In between the harsh words I suddenly saw my mother's face: she was right, I should have left before being expelled in disgrace, but the memory of her submissive face made me angry.

I interrupted him. I apologized but I was unwell, perhaps the beginning of a 'flu, I wanted to call but I found it hard to talk, and when I got home I lay on the bed and couldn't move. And in spite of all this I believe my achievements should be kept in mind. I described myself as if I was not present in the room: *an endlessly devoted teacher, thorough and well-organized,* and all these qualities had borne such beautiful fruits, as my students got the highest scores in the country.

Where did it all go wrong, turn twisted and broken? Where was the flaw that distorted and falsified the path of the righteous, making it a damaged road, full of obstacles? Had I been blind to the warning signs, ominous signals that all that appeared reasonable and clear was leading to a huge crater, visible only when standing at its brink? The principal's words echoed in the room, one word after the other, a description of errors and faults adding up to a detailed, well-reasoned verdict.

The problem is not that I left without any notice, though that is a severe violation of the regulations, but the way I conduct the lessons. My presence as a teacher is not strong enough, not to say deficient. The students feel no one is instructing them, the teacher has to be a defining person, a kind of leader, he is not afraid to say it, a charismatic personality. Though I teach well and I make sure that the students understand the material and prepare homework, this is not enough, memorizing and precision are not the heart of the teaching profession. Look at the new teacher, for example, she could set a good example for me. When she enters the classroom silence immediately prevails; the point is that the students are not afraid of her. She is both determined and relaxed, confident in her talent, and therefore the young adolescents follow her enthusiastically. And not that she is careless of the teaching itself, on the contrary, she is very meticulous, but her main advantage lies in an appropriate posture facing the class, the assertive and decisive spirit in which she directs the lesson. And by the way, yesterday she was appointed head of the grammar teaching in our school. Therefore I must meet with her so she can explain in detail what I should be teaching this year. And since lately I tend to disappear without notice, from now on I will have to report to her every time I arrive at or leave the school.

When I left the office I saw my image reflected in the wide, vitrine-like glass windows facing the principal's office: a young woman, slightly bent, limping in her twisted high-heeled shoes, her dress missing a button and a white, stained tank top poking out of it. Her hair is disheveled, the red color that covered her lips in now smeared on her chin, and her eyes are wide open, as if she was walking in darkness. One of my students passed by me; she almost greeted me but when she saw me she screamed and walked away in panic.

The ringing bell echoes in the corridors. Boys and girls are running past me, rushing to class, stampeding in a mixture of laughter and alarm, once in a while bumping into each other, giggling and swearing, and only as they see me does the stream split, and they run to either side of me, watching me with amazement and horror as I limp slowly, looking down at the ground. Finally I reach the gate and leave the school.

As I stand on the pavement I take off my shoes and walk barefoot to the bus stop. My feet are wounded; I see the scratches yet I feel nothing. The bus stop is empty, but in a couple of minute several people come, standing one behind the other. I am second in the queue. Before me is a tall man, I see his sweating back. A few women arrive, speaking in whispers. After several minutes a packed bus approaches the stop. The line advances towards the entrance door, which opens with a bang, in perfect order, but then the woman who is behind me jumps the queue and hurries to the open door, and all the other passengers follow her. If it had still been morning and I on my way to school I would have said something about the need to wait in a queue, and I would probably have added, with a smile, a couple of words about people who lack decent habits and should return to school to learn some discipline. But now I stand motionless, pushed away by a woman with shopping bags, by an elderly man with a walking stick; a teenager with headsets moving his head to the rhythm of the music hits me with his elbow, the whispering women touch me lightly and get on the bus, and after them comes a slightly dirty man with strong alcoholic breath; he bumps into me heavily and pushes me, I trip and fall down. As I raise my eyes from the pavement I see that they are all on the bus, the doors are silently closed, then the bus growls and disappears.

I am sitting on a bench. I am not sure where I am, my cell phone is right next to me. A couple of moments ago I pushed one of its buttons because it cried out and trembled for a while; Matan's voice came out of it, he was speaking constantly, neither stopping nor waiting for a response. I heard the word *fired* several times, something about the money that we need, again and again he was screaming that I should consider my moves. As his voice broke and he said he was sorry I pushed the button again, and the phone was silent. I tossed it into my bag and began to walk.

I am staggering along a long, narrow street. The sun is burning, drops of sweat roll down my back. The faces I see around me are somewhat blurred, perhaps because I am so thirsty. I look at the shop windows: elegant clothes, sweets in endless shapes, colorful ladies' lingerie. A toy shop attracts my attention. I don't know why but I enter the store. As I walk in I halt, astonished, standing with my mouth wide open in front of an endless variety of colorful trains, tiny cars, strange figures, half-man half-machine, building blocks in all tones combined in ways I have never seen before. I stand still, staring at every corner of the store, and then I see the dolls' shelves. I hasten to them like a little girl, watching them yearningly. They look like beautiful toddlers, their big eyes open with amazement, their pink cheeks rounded, and their tiny mouths slightly open, perhaps smiling, perhaps revealing adoration. For one moment the envelope of primeval, boundless darkness surrounding me is slightly ruptured. Here is a beautiful doll, her light hair glides on her neck, she is wearing a glossy purple dress. I stretch out my hand and hold her.

The face of the saleswoman is as colorful as that of the doll. She is smiling at me with obvious contempt, and doesn't conceal her disgust that a sloppy, dirty woman like me is rushing so happily to the shining toys. But I ignore her, I hold the doll carefully, sliding my hand over her pretty hair, straightening the purple dress, but then I feel there is something strange, irksome about her, something which makes me angry—but I don't know what it is; I examine her carefully, searching for the obscure fault, inspecting her meticulously from head to toe, and then I discover that on her rounded, graceful feet she has red, glossy sandals, exactly like those of the new teacher.

Once again insult and humiliation turn into physical pain, like a disease spreading fast, filling every space without leaving a single spot void of illness. I glance at the saleswoman; she is helping a mother and daughter to find a present. I turn my gaze in the opposite direction: no one is there, the store is empty. I toss the doll into my handbag, fasten the lock quickly, and turn to the entrance door. My heart is pounding, my knees are shaking, but I am careful not to drop anything, *God forbid*, so no one will notice me. A spark of childish joy is taking over me, as if I am participating in a game and am about to win, just one last sprint and I will beat the entire group; don't lose your head, keep calm, one moment and I cross the wide entrance door and step outside.

A feeling of victory overwhelms everything, submerging any dark, dreary emotion. I insert my hand into my handbag and touch the doll's hair, her muslin dress, the pleasant plastic, and I burst into short, sharp laughter. A toddler walking in the street looks at me with horror and quickly grabs his mother's hand.

How easy winning was, how perfectly simple. The fear it provoked was almost pleasant, clearing the distress and replacing it with a childish excitement, a burst of vitality I thought I had lost long ago. The thought of victory makes me so joyful, I recall with pleasure the scornful smile of the saleswoman, the shining dolls, some set on shelves, others locked in transparent boxes, the light stains on the red carpet I saw on my way out, and the striking hot air outside, the pleasant fumes rising from the steaming pavements, illuminated by a summer sun.

I take light steps, as if I was in a hurry. I don't know where I am heading but I am hungry. Here there is a bakery, I see that it is full of fresh cakes, shining in the sunlight, placed in bright straw baskets. In the store stands an elderly lady wearing a white apron, taking the fresh cakes out of the oven and putting them on the shelves. I walk into the store; the fragrance of fresh pastry is sweet and seductive. The store is crowded, people look eagerly at the glossy cakes, some cakes decorated with colorful candies, others covered with light powder. Hands are stretched out everywhere, grabbing the cakes and placing them in swishing bags, and I, too, pull out a round cake, shaped like a coiled snake. It smells of freshly ground cinnamon. I put it in a brown bag, in a moment I will stand in line for the cashier. But the desire to win is awakened again, to be in the lead, to walk past obedient clients, humble and submissive, waiting for their turn to pay, and to burst outside, to pace my way courageously to the door without revealing any weakness, my face strong and assertive, as if no one could stop me.

I am hiding the brown bag under my arm, clasping it tightly so it doesn't fall, and walking quickly to the door. When I am in the street I take out the cake, right in front of the store, before the elderly lady's eyes, and bite it deliberately, in a provocative manner. Piece after piece is ripped from the cake, and I swallow it in haste, enjoying the sweet soft dough and the crunchy top. As the last piece disappears I look at the startled elderly lady in an offensive manner and march away.

Now that I am no longer hungry I am more relaxed. Again I am walking in the street, inspecting the colorful windows. The street is full of people, shoppers holding elegant paper bags, looking at the merchandise in the windows with obvious pleasure. The memory of the meeting in school is gloomy and depressing, but on top of the sadness there is a certain joy, a light, playful spirit, it doesn't banish the sadness but it prevails in spite of it; devastating bitterness and pleasant sweetness held side by side, without disrupting each other.

Here is a men's apparel store; I watch the window. The colors are pleasant and subtle, the pants perfectly fit the shirts above them, boyish shoes are placed under elegant trousers. The garments match each other in an obscure, indistinct manner. At the center of the window there is a beautiful tie, made of fine fabric, artfully stitched, with perfect proportions. Why don't I get it for Matan? His clothes are so modest, even an inexperienced eye could see that they were purchased at a cheap department store, and though he thinks there is no difference, that all men's clothes are the same, the shabbiness of the inexpensive and over-ironed pants and shirts, with hidden traces of old stains, is evident.

When I think of Matan the hatred materializes again, detaching from the misery and becoming a separate entity, at first progressing slowly in a narrow winding lane, and then gradually drifting away into a fast, slashing stream; the way he pronounced the word 'fired' over and over again, as if it holds a hidden spiritual significance, the hints that I am irresponsible, that I act like a spoiled child, the vulgar certainty that the chain of events that led to my dismissal were merely the result of my mistakes; all these evoke anger, destroying the pleasure of the game. I hear his shrill, cracked voice as he expresses his sorrow in spite of his reservations, and then I decide I will get him the tie.

I come into the store. An elegant saleswoman is smiling at me, greeting me and asking if she can assist me. *No thanks, no need, I would like to look around.* To avoid suspicion I turn first to the shirts, looking and touching them, and then I slowly advance to the trouser shelves. Once in a while I look back. I see the saleswoman watching me, smiling as our eyes meet. I hesitate, perhaps it would be too risky and I should give up; a remote possibility that I might be caught begins to emerge, something about a paralyzing shame and nothing more. But the desire to get Matan the expensive tie, to put it on the table and watch his surprised face conceal a trace of insult, must be satisfied. My heart is pounding, my legs shake, but I don't give up. I advance to the ties counter. An abundance of shapes, colors and patterns is spread on a table. The colorful mixture makes me forget my intention for a second, but I pull myself together and begin to look for the tie I saw in the window. Here it is, at the center of the counter.

I pick it up, an elegant, shining tie—clearly it is expensive, anyone can see that. My hands are shaking, I hesitate, wondering whether I should turn around and look or just act confidently, as if it is unthinkable that I might want to steal it. My fingers slide along the fine fabric, drop it as though accidentally into my handbag. That's the way to go, drop it and immediately close the zipper, but then a deep voice is heard behind me, a salesman is asking me if I would like to purchase it. A quiet sigh of relief is coming out of my mouth, I am almost grateful, an underlying order which was violated is being re-established now, a string that was stretched to its very end, its edges torn and about to rupture, returns in an instant to its normal size, making a strange, metallic sound. Of course, I reply, I would like to purchase the tie. I follow him to the register and take the wallet out of my handbag.

The salesman wraps the tie, watching the register attentively, pushes a couple of buttons, but now he is being called to the other side of the store, he is asked to come urgently. *I am sorry*, he apologizes politely, *with your permission, one moment and I will be back.*

I took five long steps from the register to the entrance door; I grabbed the wrapped tie and rushed outside, and as I stepped on the pavement I started to run; my heartbeats were deafening, my breath lost, my legs heavy, dragging in the high-heeled shoes, twisted and injured. People look at me, a woman with entangled, wild hair and a stained dress is running as fast as she can, but I keep speeding until my strength is gone and I can't breathe anymore.

As I placed the small package wrapped in decorated paper on the table, Matan watched me, astonished. The merciful expression with which he welcomed me, compassionate but with some resentment, was gone, and instead he had a frightened countenance. *I bought you a present*, I announced with a smile, bluntly ignoring the question about where I had been until now. I removed the wrapping and held the tie in front of his wide-open eyes; in spite of the bewilderment and the reproach, a sparkle of admiration crept into his eyes, was exhibited for a second, and was gone. The bright colors, the perfect shape— the beauty of the tie was evident. Matan tried to conceal his delight, to mask the hint of a smile on his face, but once it was revealed there was no way to deny it. The satisfaction that crept into his face, slight and almost inconspicuous, made shame a pretense, nothing more. The moralizing words he meant to say in a soft, almost fatherly tone were needless and tasteless now. He stood embarrassed, lowering his gaze, neither taking the tie nor turning it down.

I smiled at him and said in a somewhat cheerful tone that I was tired, I wanted to rest, that in a couple of minutes I would go to bed. After I had dinner I returned to the room. He sat motionless in the old armchair, his back twisted and bent, his head dropped, hidden in his hands, his legs spread forward. For a moment I thought I heard a quiet groan, like a wail, but it wasn't heard again. *Matan,* I called him. He raised his head, tears covering his face, and his eyes full of alarm and horror.

Watch Dog

A line of sharp teeth, somewhat yellow, protruded from the huge, square jaws. The mouth drools a little. The heavy breathing, the erect ears—one slightly cocked to hear obscure rustles—and the big, rounded eyes indicated that the evil dog wouldn't be satisfied with a few warning barks but would leap and attack any trespassers daring to intrude into the yard. The light, wound-like stain on its forehead, the brown body with heavy muscles and a small tail, so different from the one small dogs joyfully wag, suggested how cruel his attack could be.

David watched the dog. Even though he knew that as long as he wasn't trying to open the gate and enter the yard the dog wouldn't attack him, he couldn't overcome the shaking of his hands, every finger moving at a different pace. Involuntarily he put his hands in his pockets to conceal the uncontrolled trembling, perhaps hoping to stop it, but it was hopeless; they were even more perceptible in the pockets and now they were also covered with sweat.

He felt his heartbeats, the pounding that felt like a ball tossed from within the body outwards, colliding with a strong, threatening wall that bounced the ball back. The throws became more frequent, each one stronger and more precise. His knees, normally strong and healthy, were not solid anymore, and he felt they were melting. Even though they had endured some difficult physical efforts in the past, now they could hardly carry his muscular body.

His presence in front of the gate became pointless. He tried to recall why he had agreed to come to his friend's home but could think of nothing. He couldn't make up his mind if he should call his friend and ask him to remove the threatening creature, or perhaps withdraw and return home. He stood there paralyzed and shivering, neither succumbing to the embarrassing shiver and escaping nor stepping forward.

He felt as if he had been standing there for a long time. The dog, when he realized that the uninvited visitor wasn't attempting to break into his territory, turned his gaze elsewhere, towards a nearby yard from which barking could be heard. But the shiver in David's hands didn't cease, perhaps it even increased. Now he was hesitating about what to do. Evidently a retreat would be very shameful. The dog, now standing still, would start barking, and it would be impossible to conceal his breaking away. But clearly he couldn't step forward and reach the doorbell; to do that he would have to open the gate, cross the small yard. There the dog might not only bark but attack, and his knees might collapse.

As he was standing there motionless, a loud cry came from the house. Dror, David's schoolmate, had heard the barking and came to see who was there. As he saw his friend standing at the gate he grabbed the collar around the dog's neck, opened the gate, and invited him to come in. It seemed that since he was short and somewhat chubby he would find it difficult to restrain the dog, whose growling betrayed a resentment that the uninvited guest was asked in. But feeling the fierce command of his owner, the dog stood alert and still, his muscles clearly visible beneath the thin, dark coat, gazing at David, fully focused.

David stepped inside, a forced smile on his face, asking himself if Dror could see his shaking legs and the shiver of the hands in the pockets. They had been friends since elementary school but seldom saw each other; their rare meetings took place mostly in coffee shops downtown. But this time Dror had suggested that they meet at his home since he wanted to ask his friend for his advice.

Apparently he didn't feel David's anguish. Dror smiled back, revealing thin, slightly crooked teeth, and began talking about something he had read in the paper, laughing loudly, reclining forward, yawning, and clapping his hands loudly. Immersed in the funny story, he was oblivious to his friend, pale and trembling, who had adopted a strange grimace imitating a smile. As the wild laughter decreased, he put his arm around David's shoulder, and in a friendly move pushed him to the kitchen, while inquiring if he wished to eat or drink. A moment before he boiled water to make coffee he pushed the dog out in a casual manner, as if it was a kitten, and shut the door behind it.

The sound of the slamming door brought some relief; now the distressing heartbeats decreased, again he stood firm on his feet, without fear that his knees would buckle under him. Dror was engaged in a conversation about a decision he had to make, describing to his friend the crossroads he was facing. He wanted to resume his studies after many years of driving a bus. He was not sure he would be able to learn now, it had been so many years since he graduated from high school. In fact he hadn't solved one math problem or read a scientific text for ages. But he was feeling an urge to continue his education, and hopefully he would be able to find another job. Driving a bus is exhausting. Sometimes he drives boisterous, irritating children who keep asking him endless questions and sometimes they even cut the seats, and adult passengers constantly complain about the air-conditioning. But he is not sure what he could study, and what the professional options are. His embarrassment was evident; David was thinking that his sole motivation was to avoid the dreary daily routine. He didn't mention Tami, Dror's girlfriend of the last three years, and David felt too uncomfortable to ask about her.

Faint growling was heard behind the closed door. It sounded like a complaining tone about the door being unexpectedly shut, a voice with a hint of anger, perhaps even indicating an intention to leap at the door. Then the sound of the touch of sharp claws was heard: light, creepy scratches. Dror, absorbed in contemplation of his future, got up and went towards the door with the intention of opening it. He didn't see that his friend was sweating heavily, concealing his hands in his pockets again and looking with deep fear towards the obstacle blocking the dog, which was about to be removed.

David stood up swiftly in the center of the room. He was wondering whether Dror could sense that his heart was pounding so fiercely, as if it would break out of his body, and after some hesitation gathered that his friend saw nothing, in spite of his blushing face and the sweat on his forehead. He said that he needed to leave immediately since he had to be at work at four o'clock, and mustn't be late. He was calculating what he would do if the creature burst in without Dror catching hold of it. Where would he escape to if the huge jaws should open and a line of sharp teeth be revealed? Though the growling stopped and is seemed as if the dog had gone to the next room, David was quick to say a couple of words before leaving, attempting to conceal his paralyzing terror at having to face the enormous dog. After a minute or two, he managed to escape from his friend's house and walked quickly to the nearest bus station. As he heard the gate closing behind him he felt his heart slowly returning to its normal pace, and his hands becoming still.

He often wondered when was the first time he felt the disturbing anxiety about dogs. Though he searched his childhood memories for specific incidents, he found nothing. He could remember the barks of a tiny puppy next to the nursery school, but then he was fond of dogs; he even used to pet the puppy, which often came into the nursery school, yapping in a twitting voice, running around among the toddlers. Next to his parents' apartment was a big dog, always stretched out motionless at the entrance to one of the apartments, his head resting on the doormat. Whenever anyone passed by he would open his eyes and shut them immediately, falling asleep. David was never scared of it. On the contrary, he often tried to caress it and to speak to it softly, so it would understand that he had only the best intentions. But the sleepy dog was completely indifferent to the petting and gentle words of the boy, and finally David gave up and passed by it silently. Only in adolescence did the strange anxiety emerge, but he couldn't determine exactly when it was created and why.

He recalled the piano teacher's Irish wolfhound; this dog had created the sort of unrest that precedes anxiety. As a very tall youngster, he learned that people never ascribe fear to big people. Due to his physical size everyone assumed he was brave. When the wolfhound roared, sometimes exposing its dirty teeth, the teacher assumed that David was indifferent to it and even used to joke that the dog didn't dare approach him because he is big and strong. He never suspected that the tall boy lingered for long minutes before entering the piano's teacher home, and never noticed that he moved rapidly, almost running, through the hallway and disappeared into the room where the big, black grand piano stood. But at that time, in spite of the anxiety, he could still pass next to the dog without quickening heartbeats or shivering hands.

There was also a small black poodle at the home of friends of his parents. This dog, friendly and eager to jump on visitors and lick them, was especially irksome. He went there only when his parents insisted that he join them, but often he would avoid the visit so he wouldn't have to see the curly-haired creature, leaping with joy when he saw any strangers, his sole desire being that they return some affection.

Of course, the small poodle posed no threat. If previously he used to justify his fear of dogs by thinking that they could bite or scratch, there was no doubt that this dog liked people. This made the encounter with it even more depressing: the dog leaped at him joyfully, exposing a long purple tongue, wagging his tail, expecting the visitor to greet him heartily and respond to his warm welcome with a pet, or at least with kind words.

Every visit made the encounter with the dog harder. At first there was only a light trembling in his legs, which he could easily overcome. Then it seemed as if the shiver was spreading throughout his body, perhaps even getting worse. The heartbeats became stronger, making speaking difficult. His smiles were unnatural, he spoke very loudly, almost yelling, and laughed excessively at tasteless jokes.

Once, when his parents insisted that he must go with them and he abruptly refused, he found himself left in the room with his mother. She approached him and, in a very low voice, almost whispering, asked what the true reason for his refusal was. First he said he was tired; the visit would be exhausting and it would prevent him from studying. Then he added that he was very busy, several exams at the university were scheduled for the next week. But during this conversation he recalled the dog wagging its tail, and immediately he felt his heartbeat accelerating, like a drum playing, distant but constantly approaching. Horror struck him as he realized that even the image of the dog frightened him, and he decided to tell his mother of the embarrassing anxiety about dogs.

She was somewhat surprised, but smiled and said that many people are afraid of dogs and cats, or repelled by animals in general; it is a common human reaction that shouldn't upset him. Though he insisted that it was not distaste for animals but a paralyzing fear, she dismissed his explanation and said she had often heard of such sensitivities; there was no real problem here, only a more intense response. She speculated that it might be the result of never having had a pet, or perhaps because she herself disliked animals and that had probably affected him.

His mother then recalled a niece who was scared even of fish in the aquarium, and a neighbor who had left the building because he couldn't stand the street cats sitting on the fence. Her tone became more determined: he needs to understand that most dogs don't attack humans. Big and dangerous dogs are leashed and muzzled, and small dogs wish no harm. The jolly dog of their friends really likes David, he barks because he wants to make friends with him. In a simple, straightforward tone she suggested not to avoid visiting the friends. Before entering their house, he should remind himself that the dog doesn't attack and doesn't offend people. Understanding that there was no danger would be the remedy, and he would overcome his fear; so his mother assured him.

David knew well that she was mistaken, but he was eager to believe her. The fear created simply by thinking of a dog taught him that it couldn't be eliminated by a comprehension of reality, but he was hoping it would be somewhat decreased, or at least it wouldn't be visible to others. Endlessly he tried to persuade himself that his fear is groundless, and that aggressive dogs never walk freely without a muzzle. But he learned that this understanding could not remove the alarm, perhaps only delay it a little. Yet the stories about other people dreading animals somewhat convinced him; perhaps it was possible to diminish the anxiety through self-persuasion, and to conceal it.

On Friday, a week later, his mother told him that they were planning to visit their friends on Saturday afternoon, and asked him to join them. David looked at her briefly and muttered, embarrassed, that he would come along. To avoid further conversation he returned to his room, lay on the bed, and attempted to read. His eyes skimmed through several paragraphs but he was unable to follow the sentences. The jolly dog began to materialize in his mind and he couldn't remove it. The opaque eyes covered with a film of tears, the thin curls, slightly dirty, the drizzling purple tongue: it seemed as if the dog was in his room, at his bedside, and on its face was a mocking smile. A vague feeling, which was not actually pain but could evolve to be one, appeared in his upper abdomen. He knew it well, and he could tell that when he stood up it would feel as if a part of his body was missing - the part between chest and the stomach - as if nothing supported his upper body.

David got up and began to tidy his room. The blanket tossed on the floor now covered the bed; his notebooks, always scattered on the rug, ascended to the table and gathered in its corner, the many papers jumbled on the table were squeezed into the drawer. Pens and pencils were collected from all over the room and placed in the drawer. Even the pile of books constantly resting at his bedside was transferred to the shelves, where the books were arranged according to the size of their cover, from the smallest to the largest. The drawn curtains were pushed aside and the window opened wide.

All these actions were done swiftly, one after the other, briskly and without a pause. After a couple of minutes the room was tidy, with everything in its place—only David didn't know where he could feel at ease. He sat on the edge of the bed, staring at his room as if he was a stranger, wondering what to do to eliminate, or at least to weaken, the painful feeling that spread through his upper abdomen. As he stood up he felt as if his upper body was hanging in the air. While thinking what he should do next, his heart began pounding strongly, forewarning what would happen when he faced the small dog.

Distress forced him out of the house. He went outside, saying something to his mother about going to the library, and slammed the door. He walked fast, without thinking where he was heading; after a couple of minutes he realized he was standing next to a bus station. As he was hesitating about where he should go, a young woman, a friend from the university, approached him with a smile and inquired if he had concluded an assignment that was to be submitted soon. At first he thought he would end the conversation quickly, but after a couple of sentences he felt it was distracting him from his body, pacifying him; the accelerated heartbeat decreased, the vague pain in his stomach faded, and for a minute it seemed as if fear had vanished and perhaps would never return. He therefore began to inquire at length about her life, where she came from, where she was living now, what she was studying, who her friends were. She smiled bashfully and blushed, telling him about the farm she had grown up in. David was absorbed in the stories, clinging to every detail as if it was a lifesaving rope, delving into names of friends and family members as though they masked a liberating secret.

After long minutes the friend glanced at her watch and said she was really enjoying the conversation but was in a hurry and had to leave. David was embarrassed when he realized how eager he was to talk to her. They agreed to meet soon, and he began walking again. He kept contemplating what she had told him about herself and noticed that the vague pain disappeared and his heartbeats were no more a burden. But after half an hour his body was in stress again, and the effect of the conversation with the friend expired completely.

From his return home until Saturday afternoon he was in constant torment. Cold sweat covered his back and wet his shirt, the tremor of his hands increased once in a while; he sometimes thought a part of his abdomen was missing. On the way to his parents' friends he couldn't think of anything but the future torment, the immense effort he would have to make to conceal his squirming body, and the dreadful time he would have to spend next to the detested dog, which would extend its long purple tongue towards him, naïve and indifferent to his misery.

On Saturday afternoon, he went with his parents to their friends. The fully materialized fear took hold of him without leaving the smallest, remotest room for some tranquility. His legs could hardly carry him, his hands in the pockets were completely soaked in sweat, his heartbeats filled his body, and worst of all was the attempt to conceal it all from his parents. They were immersed in a conversation on politics, which David could hardly follow. He tried to answer them with a nod or a smile so they wouldn't understand that he had no idea what they were talking about.

As they got to the friends' home, a bark came from behind the door, a sound both squeaking and grating, the source blind to the suffering it created. The door opened wide and there stood the friends and their dog. David distorted his face in an expression resembling a smile, laughed very loudly, in an exaggerated manner, at the friend's joke, and completely ignored the small dog, which was wiggling its thin tail and attempting to endear itself to the guests.

For a moment he thought he would faint. Impolitely, he walked directly to the living room without being invited in and sat in the high armchair, thinking it would be harder for the dog to reach him there. He crossed his legs so the hairy creature would face the soles of his shoes, and perhaps be repelled by them and walk away. His parents were chatting with the friends; the dog jumped and wagged his tail, leaping around the many feet. David sank into the armchair and looked at the living room as if he had never seen it before. The bookshelves against the walls appeared overloaded, as though they might collapse any moment. The blue sofa seemed to take the entire space of the room and he wondered why he and his parents sat on it so close together, clearly it had four seats. The table next to the sofa was too small in comparison to the huge pieces of furniture around it.

His parents and their friends stepped slowly to the room; following them was the curly black creature, wagging his tail, his big brown eyes look moistened with tears. David heard himself speak loudly. Distractedly he answered the questions of the friends; in spite of his attempts to appear settled and balanced he couldn't control his voice that was ascending in pitch and volume every time the dog approached him.

He spent an hour and a half in this house, wavering between fear of the creature getting close to him and dread that his shame would be exposed. True, the heartbeats decreased, the tremor of the hands was almost gone, but being in the same room with the dog was excruciating and exhausting. Before they left, he made a huge effort and stretched a hand to the puppy, which rewarded it with wet licking, but his deep sigh of relief as they finally left indicated how hard it was for him to be next to the despised creature.

Utter fatigue overtook him. One would have thought that after leaving the dog he would be relieved and perhaps even a bit happy since there was no need to control his rebellious body anymore. But instead he was completely exhausted; he felt he could hardly walk home with his parents. When they turned to him with a question he didn't reply, and once they were home he went immediately to his room, collapsed on the tidy bed, and fell deeply asleep. He woke after twelve hours.

After this visit he completely avoided all encounters with dogs. A beautiful girl with big, bright eyes was ruled out since he saw her walking a dog; a tempting job offer was rejected immediately because the employer took his wolfhound to work with him; even a meeting with childhood friends was shortened since one friend came with a gray-brown bulldog. Sometimes he was caught by surprise by an unexpected dog, but normally he would investigate who might bring a dog with him, wherever he went.

About a year and a half after the visit to his parent's friends he learned that a world-renowned expert in the field of agriculture would be coming to Israel, looking for students who would like to take part in an extensive research plan. There was nothing David wanted more. Already as a child he was attracted to the world of plants. Half-dead plants that he was trying to revive stood on his windowsill; the harder he tried the more treacherous they were. After his generous, loving watering they slowly bent to the ground and withered. He wasn't discouraged: he brought new parts of plants, placed them in glasses of water and waited for their roots to spread out, so he could plant them in flowerpots vacated by their previous inhabitants.

His love for agriculture deepened after his mother told him that his grandfather had engaged in agricultural experiments in his big yard in Eastern Europe. The grandfather used to graft one species of plant onto another, with fine results. But when the war broke out and the Nazis occupied his town, the yard was deserted. Though born after his grandfather's death, David felt he had inherited his profound understanding of the world of plants, and therefore he chose without hesitation to study agriculture at the university. As a student, plant diseases intrigued him; though they were as severe and complex as human illnesses, a lack of knowledge prevented overcoming them. He was determined to be an expert in this field and to defeat them where others had failed. He was thrilled when he heard that this world-renowned expert would be coming to

Israel for a couple of weeks. He decided to ask to meet with him, and immediately began to plan how to approach him and how he would present himself. Learning that the expert would be arriving in the third week of August, he decided to wander around the Agriculture Department office so he might meet him accidently, before the other students.

On Monday morning he arrived early, just as the secretary of the department was opening the office doors. She told him the expert should be there any minute. David waited in the hallway, rehearsing what he would say and how he would explain his profound fascination with agriculture. After a couple of minutes the expert appeared in the hallway, a man of about fifty years old, tall and thin, dressed in a somewhat elegant jacket, and next to him stepped a Dachshund dog, leashed to its owner, who was walking in an brisk and assertive manner.

The short-legged dog took David by surprise; he was unable to speak. In an instant the ball was fired from his heart, almost injuring him, his hands were trembling without control, and again he felt he was about to faint. Though his legs could hardly carry him he turned back without saying a word to the expert, hurried outside with clumsy steps, almost stumbling on a big stone, and walked away without knowing where he was going. He could see his feet moving, one foot after the other, but didn't know where they were carrying him. Next to him he saw low buildings, underneath him a gray sidewalk, but he couldn't see anything at a distance.

After a couple of minutes of accelerated walking he began to slow down, going carefully and attentively, and after a while he sat down on a bench. His heartbeats—the sharp stones his body threw at him—began to diminish, sometimes hitting the body, sometimes falling down; the spasm in the hands gradually decreased. He sat in a quiet, isolated place where no one could see or approach him, under a Margosa tree. Its rich leafy branches rustled pleasantly in a silent wind, and around him was green grass, lightly stained in yellowish gray.

The luxurious nature surrounding him made him feel somewhat at peace. He recalled the long, black dog and the horror it created, and for the first time in his life he said to himself explicitly that he is facing a difficulty that is not about to disappear. He knew that any attempt to convince himself that dogs are harmless would be futile; whenever he sees a dog he will be paralyzed by fear, even though he understands perfectly well that he is not in danger.

Now his mother's words on the fear of animals seemed pathetic and senseless. The belief that fear could be managed by an understanding of reality turned out to be ridiculous. The wisdom of life experience was disappointing: clearly she had never felt such terror and therefore couldn't perceive its unique nature. It awakens like a childhood disease, and just as the disease cannot be eliminated by self-persuasion, the anxiety exists separately from the sick child's thought. And exactly like its remote cousin, fear created by real danger, it nests in abodes remote from the peril itself.

This notion, now clear, brought him despair. He knew well how this fear was distorting and confining his life: always inquiring who would be where, and if he failed to do so he was steeped in anxiety that someone would come with a hairy, appalling creature. Whenever he knew there was a dog dwelling somewhere he had to find excuses, always miserable and hollow, why he couldn't come. And the rare cases in which he was willing to face a dog produced days, sometimes weeks, of bodily torture. Now he was sure it was not about to change; his life would always be bounded by this ridiculous and shameful terror.

While contemplating his situation, he heard a sound of steps. From his place under the shade of the Margosa tree he saw the expert walking quickly and, in front him, the small Dachshund dog, tied with a leash but pulling its owner forward. It seemed that the expert was tied to the dog and not the other way around. For a moment David thought he would hurry and approach him, but immediately the damn ball began jumping in a flurry and his hands almost tore his pockets. He tried to stand up but his legs wouldn't carry him. His sturdy body collapsed and he fell on the bench, breathing heavily, exhausted by his pounding heart.

And so, lying on the bench, unable to get up, he wondered what he should do. After long minutes of clear thinking, he decided to visit the family doctor and ask for advice.

David entered the doctor's office, self-conscious and embarrassed. He stood facing the desk, staring at an invisible spot on the wall behind the doctor, his face almost as red as his hair. The doctor concluded writing, turned his gaze to the young man standing in front of him, and asked him to sit down.

The doctor, an elderly man with a protruding stomach and heavy eyeglasses, asked David how he could help him. In spite of the practical tone, there was a touch of sarcasm in his words. David heard that doctors who treat elderly people tend to belittle the problems of younger ones, but he had never experienced it in person. He sat down and began to murmur something, and the doctor, no longer concealing his irritating smile, asked him over and over again, almost enjoying himself, what exactly his problem is.

David closed his eyes and began telling the doctor about the embarrassing fear created years ago, how often it was diverting his life to an unpredictable, unwanted path, and how deep his desire to conquer it was. He spoke for several minutes, stressing that he had overcome severe obstacles, some very demanding and difficult, but he was unable to deal with this impediment. Finally, he opened his eyes and saw that the doctor was listening intently. David stopped, waiting for him to speak.

The doctor opened with a mocking remark about the huge gap between David's muscular body and his gentle soul, but added immediately that some medications prevent these fears, and he suggested that David begin taking one immediately.

David almost snatched the prescription from the doctor's hands, and ran to the pharmacy to purchase it.

Hazy days came. At first David felt as though he was inside a glass container, sensing his surroundings from a distance. At night he would sink into a deep, distressing sleep and found it hard to wake up. But after several days his body became accustomed to the light haze, and sometimes he even found it pleasurable. He kept wondering what would happen when he next encountered a dog. After three weeks, he decided to visit his parents' friends and face the tiny creature that always wiggled its tail happily on seeing him.

He made up his mind that tomorrow afternoon he would find an excuse to pay them a visit. He would say that by chance he was near their house and was taking the opportunity to call on them. Immediately, as the decision was taken, his heart began pounding fiercely and his hands began trembling. He decided to take another pill, according to the instructions. He remembered that the doctor, examining him from behind his heavy glasses, had said that in an anxiety attack he could take two pills, perhaps even three. Now a pink capsule was taken out of the box and swallowed in haste with water.

An hour later he sank into the glass container, hearing only muffled car horns sounds and a bus passing by his house. The heartbeat decreased, he felt as if someone was catching the ball and returning it to its place before it hits the body. The tremor that always accompanied fear was almost gone; David drew his hands from his pockets, stretched them on the table and examined them at length with joy and bewilderment. They were beautiful and strong, stable and relaxed.

That evening and the next morning he was absorbed in a rigorous examination of his body; was his heart exceeding the moderate pace enforced upon it, were his hands and feet revealing impatience, was the upper part of his body well-carried, was his breath distressed? He asked his father to have his watch since it had a second hand, and checked his pulse over and over again. When his body revolted he quickly swallowed another pink pill, forcing it to yield to the medicine that was protecting him from an invisible enemy.

At noon he suddenly felt his stomach twitching lightly. For a moment his sense of confidence was shaken, he was afraid his body was about to attack him. Quickly he checked his pulse and examined his hands and feet. But the inspection revealed that nothing had changed; the twitch disappeared in a couple of minutes and his body's pumping returned to a moderate tempo.

At four o'clock he left home, walking briskly towards the bus that would carry him to his parents' friends. As he entered the bus his heart began pounding a bit faster, and again the painful ball was uprooted from its place. But David knew that the medication would tame it in about half an hour; he refrained from checking his pulse, clinging to his experience that the aching bounces would cease in minutes. And indeed, during the ride he noticed that though the pulse was a little fast, he was able to pretend that it was pounding normally.

But as he got off the bus and started walking directly to the friends' house, he felt again the familiar tremor of the palms and fingers. He stopped, pulled his hands out of his pockets and examined them at length. The involuntary moves were so apparent that he decided to put them back in the pockets, at least for a couple of minutes, so the friends wouldn't notice them. Determinedly he went up the stairs, avoiding the filthy iron handrail, ignoring the flaking walls, facing the door that hadn't been cleaned for a while, pulled his right hand from the pocket, and rang the doorbell.

The familiar barks could be heard from behind the door, along with the rattle of the dog's ridiculous collar. Apparently it leaped on the door, since David could hear light scratches on the other side. Then he heard approaching footsteps. As the woman opened the door her face filled with astonishment and joy at the unexpected visitor. She invited David to come in, pushing away the dog, leading David to the living room, inquiring if his parents were well and what brought him to this part of town.

David, fully attentive to his body, voiced the answers he had prepared in advance; he studies with someone who lives close by and his parents would be angry if they knew he passed by without coming in for a short while. As he was speaking the dog ran circles round his legs, rubbing its wretched body against them, waiting for David to stretch out his hand and pet it. David noticed that his body was reacting moderately. In spite of the accelerated heartbeats, he managed to speak without having to make an effort to conceal any shortness of breath. He saw himself reaching out and fondling the dog: first his right hand, then the left, without any noticeable quiver; his legs were firm and steady.

The dog accepted the fondling happily, shaking his tail and licking David's hands with his purple tongue. After a few minutes David felt completely at ease, as if he had never experienced an anxiety attack. It felt so pleasant that he sat down and got involved in a long conversation, and only after an hour and half stood up, made his farewells to the host, petted the dog lightly, and left.

Clean, pure wind embraced him as he passed the doorstep. He felt like a baby feeling fresh air for the first time, and was astonished by its coolness and by the way his breath was swallowed in the wind. The light seemed strong though it was twilight, and the sunset was pleasant and soft. The street, which he had seen so many times, seemed different now. For the first time he observed the tall, beautiful trees casting shadows on the old, somewhat shabby houses. A bark was heard from a house down the street, but David didn't even look to see where it was coming from.

After two weeks of visiting friends with dogs, he decided it was time to try to meet the expert. He went to the department office and asked the secretary how he could meet him. She replied that it so happened that today he was inviting several students to his home, in a neighborhood at some distance from the university. She suggested that David join them, and added, smiling, that hopefully this time he would be able to face the expert. David ignored the allusion to his escape from the previous encounter and asked when the students were invited for.

The thought of the few hours left until the meeting displaced the ball, and it began rocking to and forth forcefully. Even his hands, which hadn't trembled for days, began to move, and again he had to tuck them in his pockets. Immediately he looked for the pink capsules; as soon as he found them he swallowed one and, after some hesitation, put four pills in his pockets. For half an hour he paced rapidly in his room, unable to stop. For a moment he thought that if he halted the ball would really break out of his body, his knees wouldn't be able to hold him, and he would collapse. But after a couple of minutes his pulse decreased, the hands didn't move anymore, and his knees steadied. When he felt that his body could be still, he sat comfortably in the armchair in his room.

After two hours he awoke, surprised that he had fallen asleep, and now he felt somewhat stronger. He began preparing for the ride to the expert's home. He put some research plans in his backpack, added a small bottle of water, and left.

When he reached the neighborhood, he realized he didn't know where the street he was looking for was. Small houses surrounded by gardens were scattered on the mountainside, and the narrow streets were empty. He walked downhill under tall trees, searching for the address the secretary had given him. After a couple of minutes of walking, he saw, at a distance, three students standing in front of a house, looking into its yard. David assumed they were waiting for their friends, so they would all enter together. But as he approached them, he noticed they were whispering and pointing at something behind the fence. After a few steps he joined them, and then he realized why they were standing still without ringing the doorbell.

An immense creature, almost as high as David's waist, stood behind the gate making threatening growls, with a transparent dribble coming out of his mouth. His brown, thorny coat, which was a bit dirty, emphasized the strong, rounded muscles in his back and front legs. But in spite of their size it seemed as if they could hardly support the steel-like, powerful body. The front fur was blond, at its heart a red-black stain, like an apron dirtied with the victim's blood. Its face was daunting: square jaws revealing restrained evil, wise eyes calculating the enemy's weakness, a huge black nose, so big that the constant movement of the nostril was visible, detecting the odor of a prey. It was his cropped ears that gave his face a softer, almost human expression, perhaps because they seemed wounded. But even though they looked like little more than the remnants of canine ears they moved constantly from side to side at the sound of any murmur. But more intimidating than anything was his posture, for although resting motionless on his paws, his body seemed in the midst of a huge leap at an invisible enemy. He stood still, except for the outstretched tongue that moved in the rhythm of his breath, but his muscles were fully strained. The thin long tail, so unsuited to the stout body, perhaps a remnant of a more gentle breed, was motionless, so as not to impede the stationary jump of this dog.

David looked at it with both fear and astonishment; he had never seen such a giant hound. Though he was very familiar with the fear awakened by the presence of a dog, he saw at once that this creature had something beyond the distortion created by anxiety. Simultaneously with the ball that was immediately shot against his body, and the pockets wet from the heavy sweating, a sigh of relief came out his mouth—almost a cry. Anyone with eyes could see that this was not an absurd panic to be overcome, but fear of a real, tangible danger. The immense dog would dismember any trespasser with its forceful jaws. He looked back at the other students, seeking confirmation, but as he turned his head he saw that they had left, and he was facing the massive creature by himself.

To his utmost surprise he felt a compelling urge to act. Normally, anxiety would awaken his internal organs but paralyze the exterior part of his body. He used to think of himself as a frozen man, waiting to defrost so that he could move. But this time he was completely alert; every single muscle of his hands and legs refused to escape from the fearful dog. As he was contemplating what he should do, he observed that the ball bouncing within his body was gradually slowing down and the palms of his hands were dry. He opened the gate and stepped cautiously into the yard. He looked down and saw a big, leafless branch on the ground. He drew his hand out of his pocket, bent down, picked it up, and with a quick, threatening motion waved it at the giant creature, as if he was trying to hit it.

The dog emitted a restrained roar, which sounded like it was coming from his abdomen and not from his mouth, and looked at the stick. Its alert body didn't retract at all, but he seemed surprised, perhaps even disappointed, by the strange enemy that appeared today. Its immense nose approached the branch, scornfully smelling the weapon so unbecoming to his size, moving only the right nostril. Even though his body remained still, the thin tail began wagging, as if David and his branch were nothing but a light amusement.

It was evident that threatening the dog was pointless. Its restrained reaction to the branch waved at it indicated how strong it was. Perhaps it was trained to avoid useless scuffles with inferior enemies. It growled again, looked directly at David as if wondering what he would do next, his tail not wiggling anymore but dropped behind his back.

Suddenly the voice of the expert came from the house. Apparently he was on the phone; he spoke loudly, in fluent English, giggling nervously once in a while and coughing afterwards. David attempted to overhear the conversation, but all he could comprehend were some technical terms in agriculture. Then he said something about a student he was expecting, some 'project', and then the expert began laughing loudly.

As David heard that, he bent slightly forward and determinedly turned his gaze from the dog to the ground; he began walking towards the door as if he was unaware of the huge creature about to leap on him and bite him with its sharp teeth. He took small, even steps, looking downward, exploring every small plant or dry thorn as if they were immense obstacles, extremely difficult to surpass. Again he could feel his heartbeats, which time and again had overpowered him: but this time he was determined not to withdraw. Though he was a cautious, well-balanced person, a strange mood took over him now, an odd mixture of frenzy and full confidence in fate. Like a circus acrobat, jumping from a high springboard to grab the hand of another acrobat at a precisely-calculated moment, clinging to his friend so he won't crash, his heart thudding fearsomely, but knowing that salvation depends on a blind belief in fate, so did David walk towards the door.

The giant dog seemed taken by surprise by the determination of his enemy. It took a step backwards, its muscles becoming tighter, made another restrained growl, attempting to inspect the strange intruder who walked in such miniature steps that one foot touched the other while his gaze turned to the ground, ignoring the immense dog as if it was a tiny poodle. He didn't resemble his vigorous owner, who dominated him in a casual manner, and he seemed different from the strange characters surrounding the yard, looking at him with hatred and fear and running away when they heard his growls. This man's face betrayed an immense effort, yet he kept moving forward as though no power in the world could stop him.

David halted. The ball within his body was becoming tender. Though he felt it well, its touch was more like fondling, as if it was a canvas ball toddlers play with; for a moment he thought he could hear the small bells ringing inside it. His knees were soft, but suddenly they seemed flexible, as if they could bend easily and then straighten again. The fear that his legs wouldn't carry him was somehow transformed into a confidence that if they did fold, he could easily unfold them and walk. But looking at his hands, which always betrayed him, he was truly amazed: they were peaceful and stable, resting in his pockets that felt like soft leather gloves coating the hands.

Slowly he raised his eyes and looked straight at the dog; at the thin paws with their black, sharp claws; at the strong body with the stain at its heart; at the muscular jaws, at the big black nose, and at the eyes that watched him with amazement and suspicion. One couldn't ignore the fact that this immense dog is hesitant and doesn't know what to do. Should it attack the strange trespasser or let him go?

Finally, like all hesitant dogs, it began to bark. A tone resembling a scream came out of its mouth, a machine-like sound, not the voice of a living creature. It was a metallic bark lacking any grumble, an impartial echo. He hardly opened his mouth to yelp, it seemed to come from within his muscular body, but could be heard only because his jaws weren't tightly closed. It barked over and over again, neither withdrawing nor stepping forward; a withdrawal would have been an admission of defeat, but it was impossible to tell if an attack would be successful. Its legs stuck in the ground, the big dog stood motionless and barked, perhaps with the hope that the noise would implant fear in the heart of the intruder.

When David saw the dog was barking, he knew he shouldn't halt; if it was sure of its triumph it would leap and attack him. David took large, vigorous steps, quickly evaded a thorny plant, went by a blooming geranium, and turned towards the dog. In spite of its husky barking David approached it, and when only one small shrub stood between them he stretched his hand toward it.

A long palm approached the immense animal without a trace of quiver, the gentle fingers inviting the dog to smell them, to acknowledge the triumph of the intruder and clear the way. The dog looked at a pair of athletic legs; in spite of a very slight movement around the knees they held the body easily. And from the blue eyes that watched him, triumphant drops splattered. The palm of the hand was still, enjoying the noisy sniffing without recoil, forcing the dog to admit that not only had it not attacked the intruder but now it was also adjusting to his scent.

The dog's body shook in agitation. His muscular feet moved constantly, one after the other, like a soldier marching in place. It looked like an animal pressed into a trap and now hesitating whether to attack in order to escape. The square jaws were somewhat loose, the eyes examined the trespasser with fear and confusion, and the ears were turned to David, to hear any sound he might make.

The bouncing ball in David's chest became so gentle, almost imperceptible, touching him like a feather. His breathing was comfortable and relaxed, the hand touching the dog didn't reveal its inner tremor, which might nonetheless break out unexpectedly. David waited for a while and then lifted his hand and touched the dog's forehead, not petting it but establishing his authority.

Then he looked at the expert's house and began to walk towards it with confidence, not watching the dog, which turned around and moved in the direction of the fence, its head bent down and its strong muscles loose as if it was injured. After a few steps on the stony pathway, David raised his hand to ring the doorbell, but before he touched the bell the expert opened the door. He was dressed very casually and his cheeks were covered with gray bristles. He smiled pleasantly at David and said that he sees he is the only student who came, or maybe the others gave up and left, but please, come in, he has plenty of free time now. He made an inviting gesture with his hand, then followed David into the house, and closed the heavy wooden door behind him, leaving the big dog recumbent in the yard, its heavy head lying motionless on the wet ground and its eyes closed.

Aura

A dim grayish light is in the distance. Maybe it is coming from a remote streetlight, maybe from a reflection of light on water. Squinting makes it possible to see that the heart of the light is more intense, and around it there is an aura, beams of light spattered and spreading everywhere. But since it is in the distance it is hard to see the details.

I don't understand, the core seems only a couple of steps away from me but the aura is remote and blurred, like a star at the end of the sky, which can only be seen in the rare moments of cloudlessness. I try to understand where this huge beam is coming from but all my attempts to follow it are in vain. I notice that the stream of light is oscillating from side to side, but how come the core remains motionless while the beams escape each other, every ray moving at a different pace and towards a different direction?

Now I realize the light is in a strange space, like a long tunnel; its end cannot be seen. Again I squint, wishing to find its head, to see what is beyond it. But all I can see is a stain, perhaps silver perhaps gray, touched with white spots, a formless body, constantly changing, like a cloud on a winter's day, advancing in haste and transforming all the time, adopting a form and then at once altering it. For a moment I believe I have managed to capture its form, holding it within me, but it disappears and immediately another form emerges, strange and indistinct. There is no knowing whether it is reflection or source, sun or moon.

Despair takes over me; I don't know where I am and what the strange lights are. Can I walk towards them? While I am considering what to do I realize that I can't move. I try to take one step forward, but my legs don't obey. The light is flashing in front of me yet I can't approach it. I try to figure out why, but then a storm overwhelms me, I believe heavy winds are blowing here and soon I will fly with them. Something is rocking me, I feel as if I am lifted and then I fall down with a bang, which is both pleasant and repulsive. Maybe I should cling to something so that I don't fall; but as I try to do so I realize again that I can't move. Not that I can't feel my body, on the contrary, I feel as heavy as if I were carved in stone, and I simply don't have enough strength to move.

As I am thinking what I should do, I vaguely hear voices. One sounds like a whistling wind, a soft rumbling, a breeze filtering into clefts and then exiting with a soft sigh. I follow the voice of the wind and then I find it is not alone, it is submerged in another voice, lower and segmented like the hoot of a night bird, perhaps an owl, crying out loud and then silent until the next cry. The cries of this bird blend with the rumbling of the wind, then I notice another voice, high and delicate. I try to follow it but can rarely hear it. Once in a while it creeps into the ear, the sound of a gentle flute, pure and unornamented. I am tense, exerting myself to hear the flute in the distance, wondering where it is coming from; for a moment I think it is to my side but then it recedes and diminishes, finally sounding as if it is coming from behind high summits, or perhaps even beyond the river.

I know I am close to a river, or maybe a sea. I hear the flowing water: sometimes slow and moderate, at other times splashing, breaking on a rock and then falling down, drawn into a huge vortex leading to the bottom of the sea. I love the sound of water. Though I am probably on land, listening to the waves I feel I am floating. Drops splash on my body and make me wet. The rumble of the moving water makes me ignore the other voices since it is constant and quiet, like a sound familiar from years ago—I don't know when I have heard it but it is so pleasant, I know the water is warm though I never touch it.

I think the light is changing. Maybe it is after sunset, I am not sure, but something pale and unpleasant is shedding its light around me. Again I try to follow the gleam, but now it is better defined, constant, and not appearing and disappearing again. Is this a full moon night? I don't think so, since moonlight is so pleasant, caressing, with golden white rays, whereas this light is oppressive and somewhat bluish, leaving no room for any shade in which to relax. I strain my eyes to see better; I see everything from behind a screen, I don't understand what it is. I realize that all my efforts to find out where I am are in vain since something is standing between me and the lights and sounds. A membrane-like material surrounds me, brownish gray, spotted and slightly perforated, pieces of broken skin here and there, and now I also see thin burgundy lines, intertwined and merging into each other, beginning very low and stretching all the way up, to a place where I can't see them anymore. I follow these red rivers, watch how one splits from the other and then breaks up into small brooks, ending with a curve. I find this place strange, I don't understand where I am. Am I lost in a cave? Perhaps. I also feel a strange scent, maybe it is mildew on the wall of the cave, something which reminds me of old wine, but without its warm sweetness.

Ah, the oppressive light is off, how nice. Now it is almost completely dark, except for a small glimmer on the side. The voices also are gone, I can't hear anything besides a constant dripping, probably water dropping on the walls of the cave. Every second a drop falls and hits the floor; it makes a subtle sound, extremely delicate, a light breaking of water, splashing with an almost inaudible ring. I am relieved, I don't like the distant light, it reminds me that I am in the heart of a deep cave and I don't know if I will ever be able to escape it.

Suddenly I am appalled by a horrible sound. Wheels make a deafening scream, there is a blast of iron crashing into something and bending, ravens crying out in a deafening voice, light blood splashing everywhere, a falcon is swooping from above to grab a poisonous snake, pulling me with it, I cling to its wings between sky and earth, gripping it as tightly as I can so I won't crash, but the falcon holds the snake and shakes me off its wings and I am thrown to the ground and hit it. At first I don't feel my body, but then a terrible, blinding pain engulfs me, my body is torn from itself and I am dismembered; from a distance I hear the continuous wailing, ascending and descending, of a hungry, exhausted jackal.

I am in the same tunnel, but now it seems shorter and wider. The light emerging from the entrance is clearer, as if it has an intrinsic logic, the space is extending closer to the aura. I see that the beams move in one direction at a constant pace: the chaos is gone and a new order has been created, something that can be perceived by the senses. No doubt I am closer to the entrance of the tunnel, I can feel it clearly, but now the voices emerging from the other side are different. I think a mother bear is growling there, a deep, warm voice, constant and unbroken, more like a blow of hot air than an animal's voice. The growling is very pleasant, for a moment I am afraid it will cease, but mother bear doesn't let go, she emits her good voice again and again, like an oboe which, rather than sounding like something external, feels like a voice existing within itself. And then, to my utter surprise, the chilly nose of the bear touches me. It feels pleasant and soft, a bit wet, touching my cheek like a kiss. I think the bear is not sure whether her nose is touching me or not.

The smell is also better. The old wine is spilled and gone, and instead there is a scent of flowers. I am trying to guess which flowers grow on the other side, but cannot. For a moment I think I smell daffodils, but immediately it becomes clear that the scent is more delicate; it is carried on light air and fades. Chrysanthemum? I don't know. The odor is pleasant though hard to sense in full. I want to inhale it again but it is gone.

As I am absorbed by the bear's faint, soft growls, I suddenly hear the owl's voice again, hoarse and fragmented, making a noise as if it is sitting on a tree looking down at me with utter surprise, wondering what brought me to this place.

And then, unexpectedly, a huge surge of water flows over the strange membrane around me; a turbid wave surrounds me completely, warm and a bit salty, advancing to the shore. Apparently the sea is rough, since the water is splashing everywhere and I find it hard to breathe. The growls of the bear are submerged in the sound of the water, and I ask myself if I am about to sink to the bottom of the sea. I think not, since the light remains unchanged. I struggle with the water around me but then, in an instant, it flows away to the land, leaving me breathless and alert, anticipating the next wave. But after a couple of seconds I realize it is low tide now, the water is gone until high tide returns. I relax, the palms of my hands open a bit, my hands sink back, but then—

A noise of wheels abruptly coming to a halt stuns me. There is a strong smell of burnt rubber. Painful cries are heard everywhere, I don't know who is screaming. My eyes are covered with a crust of dried blood, I can't open them, my body is wide open and my organs are spread around me. A huge ant is crawling on me and I can't get rid of it, it approaches my face, touches the right nostril and I am in panic, soon it will be inside me. I try to call for help, there must be someone who can hear me, but instead of my voice a strange snort comes out of my mouth, a weird mixture of choking and laughter, a voice saturated with blood and water.

Again I feel the oppressive blue light. A white luster surrounds me. I am out of the tunnel, I know this for sure. All those remote lights are frighteningly close now—I can almost touch them. If I were to move my head carelessly they would hit me. The strange membrane around me seems almost transparent, and now I see it is also perforated with needle-eye-sized holes. The red brooks are thin and narrow, delicate threads that emerge from an unknown place and then disappear.

I am stricken with horror: the membrane is torn in two places, there are two long cracks in the screen, spoiling the pleasant warmth around me, I am exposed, I don't know where I can escape to, the ruptures are becoming rounder, I am afraid the lights will permeate through me, I try to stop the widening of the tears but fail to do so. They are becoming bigger every moment, blown into huge spheres, somewhat elliptical; an intense light penetrates me, shocking me, I feel as though I am lying on a lab table and being moved from one side to the other. I look for some shade but can't find any, everything is disgustingly lit. Perhaps I could find a tree and hide between its leaves, or a small shack on a side road which I could get into, drop on a bench, and stare at the empty walls; or maybe a small flaking boat, its oars rusty, but still able to be pushed to the water, and I could lie in it and let the steam carry me with it. I watch the elongated spheres with horror and see they are surrounded by black protuberances, like small, rounded hairs, tiny snakes stuck in their place and unable to move away. They don't conceal the cracks but rather emphasize them. If I could,

I would escape from this place, abandon these oppressing lights lacking the slightest compassion, penetrating me, ignoring the pain they cause, attempting to illuminate without mercy what should be left in the dark. Even if they can be endured for a minute, this beam of light leaves me breathless, suffocated by a desire to throw myself into the darkness.

The voice of the bear is still echoing, sweet and warm, and then I feel it is materializing in front of me. I try hard to see its contours but the figure I see is incomprehensible. The bear is bald, I think she has lost almost all her body hair except for some strange locks on her head, each one facing a different direction. Her eyes are brown and round, watching me with deep concentration, as if I am about to say something very important: she is waiting for me to speak. Her face has deep furrows, her skin looks rigid, as if she had just been extracted from the bottom of the sea. Her mouth is wide open, her face reveals her painful excitement. She cries out. I don't understand what she is saying but now her voice is low and harsh. I look at her, hallucinating, and then I understand it is a woman that I see.

She bends over me, caressing my face. Her hands, blocks of unchiselled chalk, are scratching me. I look at her in horror: her eyes are wet, tears gliding along the deep slots, her mouth is shivering and she keeps repeating *Gil, Gil, Gil.* I don't understand what she is saying: she is repeating this syllable as if it holds a secret, as if pronouncing it would reveal the secret of my being in this place.

I am in a strange place, everything is painfully dazzling. Various metals surround me, I am lying on a bed floating in air. I can't see what is underneath it, but the weirdest thing is that everything is snow-white here, the walls, the closets, the bed, the table, as if an evil spirit had passed through and taken all the colors with it, and all that was left is an irksome white, leaving no room for joy. Transparent tubes cover me, surrounding me and threatening to suffocate me. Now I see that my hands are placed at my sides, perforated with strange nails, stuck in my palms, my arms, and probably my legs as well. I am placed on a bed, resembling a cadaver more than a living man; my head is a slightly raised, I don't know why, but I feel pain in my neck, as if someone is holding me fiercely and won't let go, forcing me to laugh and cry. And this strange woman is standing next to me and screaming *Gil Gil Gil*, as if the cry itself might bring some relief.

I close my eyes; with all my heart I desire to return to the cave I have left. I miss the smell of mildew, the darkness, the light sound of water drops bouncing on the walls of the cave, and the wide sea next to it. Maybe the high tide will come and rescue me from this white place. But no, nothing will save me from this horrible bed that is floating in the air and the dreadful woman: her sole desire is that I say something, she is completely indifferent to my wishes and only wants me to gratify her. I understand she thinks I can't hear her and therefore she is shouting her strange words, hoping perhaps that the entire membrane will break and I will be torn from myself, to become a huge warm clod of earth: as I would like to be.

Now a man appears, wearing a green shirt, a sort of color I have never seen before, like the sky during sunset but lacking the warmth of the sun, and he is looking at me curiously. He offers a couple of fragmented words, one word – stop – another word – and then he draws a small flashlight from his pocket, opens my eyes and puts the flashlight a finger away from the pupil of one eye. A catastrophic light floods me, I never knew it was possible to drown in light and now I am suffocating, my breath is arrested, the light is blinding. I can't see anything and a different whiteness surrounds me, mortifying, debasing, deforming. Once again I am assailed by the smell of burning tires, I am hurled onto boiling iron pipes and my body is melting in the heat, the organs are ripped away; I want to cry but a snort emerges, and then I am lying on the earth, its good smell—a steamy scent of mud clods after a heavy rain—slightly eases my pain.

I open my eyes again. The old lady is sitting next to me, watching me yearningly, as if I have a secret which, if I share it with her, it will dispel all her misery. She holds my hand and fondles it but her touch is so rough that I find it hard to bear. A clay hand is sliding on my cheek, trying to touch my lips, but stops at the last moment and lets me go. I think I saw her once, a long time ago, maybe when I was in the cave, perhaps even before that. Her face seems so familiar: the round brown eyes, the sharp nose, the sagging, wrinkled cheeks, the thin mouth, slightly open, pulled upwards on one side, and the disheveled hair, every lock turning in a different direction. She gets up, leans towards me so I can hear her well, points a finger at herself and overemphasizing the words says: *mommy, mommy, mommy.*

Apparently it is night since the blue light is off, and now a lamp spreads a pleasant glow in the room. It makes the lack of color less burdening. A curtain blowing in the wind casts gray shadows, moving at a constant pace above the bed as it floats in the air. It lifts up, stretches to the side in a soft movement, and then nestles against the wall. A lovely wind touches my face, carrying a scent of wet leaves after rain. I look out the window and in the darkness I see a damp tree; the wind is shedding tiny, transparent raindrops from it. Suddenly a short woman enters the room. Her hair is pulled behind her head and her face is somber. She approaches the bed. I am anxious, I don't know her, but to my utter surprise she holds the parchment standing at the head of the bed and reads it as if it were a mysterious, enigmatic script. I watch her, immersed in reading, surprised by her majestic outfit, a dark purple suit which is as gloomy as her. When she is done reading she approaches, glances at me shortly as if I were a huge lizard lying on the bed, and says: *Gil? Are you Gil? Can you hear me? Can you hear me? Gil?*

Gil. This is what they call me here. I don't know why, but this is how people address me. The older woman, the short woman dressed in purple, also the man whose clothes are the color of the sky, they all roll the word on their tongues as if it was the solution to a riddle. They put their faces next to my ears, as if I can't hear them when they stand in front of me. The man dressed in blue has eyeglasses. I recognize his voice, he says a word—stops—and then comes another one. He doesn't blind me with the flashlight anymore. Now he holds my palm fiercely, his hands are strong and stable, confident and certain; he presses his finger on my wrist and closes his eyes, as if music is coming out of my hand and he is eager to listen to it. In spite of the pain he generates he seems extremely satisfied, as if at this very moment he has finally understood the hidden link between my palm and an old tune.

The older woman, the one that looks somewhat familiar, and the man are whispering to each other. By their expression I can tell they are trying to conceal something from me, hinting and winking, then walking away from my bed. They watch me with a worried look. I feel I need to do something to satisfy them, but I don't know what. The man is showing a piece of paper to the woman and they are at once both immersed in it, reading every line; once in a while they look at me as if I knew what was written there, but I let them down time and again.

Apparently I fell asleep; now, when I open my eyes, the man and the woman are gone and I feel there is no one around. The only thing I can hear is faint voices in the distance. Then I feel something like a sting in my arm. My organs are so heavy I think they are made of stone. The stings don't stop, again and again, light and cutting, they feel like tickling, reminding me of a childish pinch. I am trying to look aside, my neck is aching as if it was placed in a cast with sharp wheels, but I am determined to turn it. Slowly I roll my neck, and I see, standing beside me, a little girl. Her beauty is dazzling, like a precious stone; I can't take my eyes off her: straight chestnut hair, falling almost to her waist, assuming a graceful curl at its ends; her lips are full, her brown, innocent eyes are examining me with childish curiosity, but the heart of her charm is the straight, light eyebrows, thick golden stripes—lacking the normal curve of an eyebrow, they look like gentle paintbrush strokes in the lightest possible brown, full soft lines of pure wonder.

She is standing by my bedside. Her head is so close to mine that I almost feel her breath, watching me and hesitating what to say. She lets go of my arm and now she stretches a childish finger toward my face, dabbing my cheek with a light caress, almost imperceptible, like a feather's touch. My heart is palpitating. I wonder how this creature happened to come here, she would fit better in the cave and in the sea surrounding it than in the crystal white room, but now she is bending towards me, her hair touches my body, and in a voice revealing both wonder and complaint she says:

Daddy? Daddy?!

I want to answer her, to say something, to ask who she is, but I turn mute; I am unable to pronounce syllables, only warm breath is coming out of my mouth. The girl looks at me amazed, trying to follow the strange sounds I make, then a light smile spreads on her lips. She seems somewhat amused by my attempts to speak. Again she sends a childish hand, rounded, dimpled, towards me: she touches my cheeks, my lips, sliding her finger on my nose, circling around it, and stopping at the chin, and then the beautiful face is filled with a huge smile, her pretty eyebrows are stretched slightly, her eyes are shining, and she says: *what happened to you in the accident?*

There is a blaring sound, I close my eyes and shrink, the girl disappears, and I inhale the smell of burnt rubber again, there is something passing above and dropping into the valley beneath me. I am on a gray rock, between sky and earth, I must cling to something so I won't fall, but the burning iron which I clutch with all my strength is curving and bending. Together with it I sink down: it is impossible to fall for such a long time before hitting the ground, but when I crash on the earth my body is a mixture of blood, soil, and burning metal parts, stuck within me as if they were intended to stop my body from shattering.

Night. I am dizzy. I just woke up. I feel like the room is moving slightly, the walls tilting upward and the bed downward. The straight lines of the closet are not as sharp as they were. Now they are somewhat rounded and the gray handles are not in their place, some are too low, others too high. The curtain that is now motionless seems a bit distorted. Its pleats are horizontal, but it is impossible that with the wind blowing so hard here the curtain doesn't move. I think perhaps I have returned to the cave again but then I see the elderly woman, my mother, standing next to me and watching me. Her face is anxious, she murmurs something quietly, she is extremely pale and she holds the bed so she won't collapse.

After a couple of moments of silence she says: *Gil, how are you? Better?* I see she is trembling, with all my heart I would like to please her, to say something that would make her happy, but I don't know what. An old, bitter woman, extremely agitated. A fishing-net of wrinkles has caught her face, she clings to the bed in exhaustion, waiting for me to recognize her, to call her *mommy.*

As I open my mouth and try to talk, the door opens. A younger woman is entering, stepping carefully into the room and advancing on the tips of her toes to the bed. She approaches me, leans forward and looks at me. In her green eyes tiny brown islands are floating, curly black hair surrounds her thin face; she exudes a strange mixture of happiness and sadness. As she watches me she tries to catch my eyes, as though if I looked at her she could rescue me from this torment. I look straight into the green-brown luminous balls, and I don't know if they are covered with tears or by a luster of affection. She smiles at me, and like everyone else she says: *Gil, Gil, Gil,* as if this syllable has magic that will act immediately. I find it hard to focus my gaze, again I feel a deep pain in my neck, as if sharp wheels are supporting it. She holds my hand, and then I realize it is no longer perforated with nails but placed next to me smooth and clean. Yet her touch is demanding, she wants me to watch her with shining eyes too. However I, more than anything, would like to sleep, to close my eyes and return to the good, soft cave: its dim light is so pleasant, ivy covers its walls, and the sound of dripping water is as good and delicate as could possibly be. But I can't, she grabs my hand, forcing herself to smile at me, fondling my face with thin, long fingers with red stains at their ends, and then she stands erect, turns around, and walks to the door. A thin woman, elegantly dressed, walking on high heels, her face made up; but I see a young girl, it seems to me that in a moment she will open her shining purse, take out a lollipop, and lick it eagerly.

In the morning the somber woman appears, her face a symbol of endless devotion. Once again she is absorbed in the parchment, to which she adds some notes. After her comes the man in blue clothes; this morning he is especially haughty. He approaches me, pats my arm lightly and says: *how are you Gil? I am the doctor.* Now I understand he is a physician, and clearly I am ill. I know my body parts are painfully heavy and I can't move. He explains something in a serious voice, I can't follow what he is saying but he points at my head, touches it lightly, moves it from side to side, nods with satisfaction, and walks away.

Later my mother comes. She looks at me with surprise, I don't know why; apparently something in my appearance has changed. She is determined to conceal her embarrassment, perhaps even aversion, but unintentionally her eyes examine my forehead, my skull, my ears, as if they were completely altered. After a couple of minutes of looking at me I hear her say the word *surgery.* Thin, transparent tears come out of her eyes and gather into the narrow canals engraved in her face. I feel sorry for her; I know I saw her many years ago, but I can hardly remember anything. I see how my illness torments her: her agony is so clear, she doesn't even attempt to dry the tears, only looks at me as if she was seeing me now for the first time. Happily the girl bursts into the room—but she stops abruptly, looks at me terrified: in a moment she will escape in panic, her beautiful face is twitching, her innocent eyes are wide open, her mouth is tightly closed, and then she says: *daddy, why are you bald?*

Last comes the young woman. Today her dark hair is piled behind her head and her face can be seen clearly. She has a weird mixture of adolescence and old age, the shyness of a girl and the contemplative expression born of the experiences of a long life. Her face is already somewhat wrinkled, but still she is made up like a young girl who dares to color her face for the first time; the color is not meant to beautify her but to indicate that she is a woman. As she looks at me she is so shocked she can't hide her disgust, but then she gets a grip on herself and smiles, saying: *Gil, where is your hair?*

She sits beside me on the bed, her fingers touch my arms and I feel that my stony body parts are becoming lighter. She fastens the buttons of the strange shirt I am wearing, a kind of green robe with a pocket. Her manner clearly reveals that she feels my body belongs to her and she is used to touching it—she doesn't hesitate for a single moment, she sits down beside me, runs the gentle fingers with red spots over my arm. Her touch is so pleasant: now she caresses my face, my neck, my chest, I can feel her warmth through the robe, her softness, I see she is very careful not to hurt me, avoiding the wounds under the heavy, uncomfortable bandages. I close my eyes, hoping she won't stop, giving in to the light hand running all through my body. As I open my eyes I see she is watching me with concentration and then says: *Gil, do you remember me? Do you know who I am?*

In an instance the magic is gone, her hand is burdensome, I am waiting for her to take it off. Know her? I have no idea who she is. True, there is something familiar about her face, I can't deny it—something about the lips, maybe the way she compresses them, the upper one a bit rigid, the lower one round and protruding—as if I had seen her photo in a postcard or a newspaper, but of course I don't know who she is. She is expecting me to acknowledge what seems to her clear and evident. *Gil? Do you recall?* she asks. If my hands were lighter I would push her off the bed and away from this white room. Her caresses are so pleasant, but now she wants me to please her, to admit an affinity between us, and I have no idea who she is. Her insistence is revolting, annoying. I am trying to move my hand but then I think I hear a terrible cry, a scream, like the one the eagle made as he dived down and threw me off his wings to the abyss, I am hot, I can't stand this fire, my heart is pounding strongly, I am choking—

Night. The women and the girl are finally gone. I couldn't stand their faces for another second. I feel suffocated when they are here: I wait for the moment in which they will wave their hands kindly, with a big smile to illustrate how much they like me, say a couple of warm words, sometimes even with a friendly, casual touch, and leave. I sigh with relief, no one is asking me to pretend that we are related by an unbreakable bond. The quiet of the night is good for me. I rest, listening to the wind outside. Sometimes the window is left open and the scent of fresh rain on trees spreads, diminishing the impression of the white room and of all those who wish me well. And so in my imagination I can travel to other places. Sometimes I hear a cat meowing, a night bird tweeting, I listen to these voices with utter pleasure. The sound of rain splashing on my window is delightful, a gentle, soft tapping; sometimes I feel it is washing me and cleansing the room of the depressing smell.

A new woman appears; now I understand she is a night-shift nurse. A tall woman, with big blue eyes, elegantly dressed, a face that looks generous and kind. But in spite of the smile in her eyes she is more determined to do her job than any other nurse, eager to put needles in my body again and again. Pain makes me cry, sometimes I even scream, but nothing distracts her from her job. I know she doesn't stop for a second, she has resolved to fulfill her obligations and nurse me. Sometimes I watch her holding the needles, immersed in inserting a tube into my arm and believe that had she been forbidden to take care of patients she would have felt completely at a loss; her countenance attests that she came into this world in order help the sick and to ease their pain. When she is done sucking the bubbling blood, she smiles pleasantly, sometimes even winks at me, and then says in a quiet, relaxed voice: *good night, Gil, I hope you sleep well.*

But I don't sleep. And tonight a surprise comes along. As I am thinking about the cave and trying to revive its scent, an unknown woman suddenly enters the room. I see she doesn't belong here, she isn't wearing a uniform but blue pants and a grayish-pink sweater. It is already early morning, the dawn rays clear the darkness, the night-shift nurses are tired and they don't see that a strange woman is coming into the patients' rooms. She is looking at me. I have never seen such soft eyes, she watches me with a mixture of sympathy and pity. Obviously she is looking for someone and doesn't expect anyone to be awake at this early morning hour. To my astonishment I find I am smiling at her. Even my voice, now really coming out of my mouth, greets her. She is surprised too, taken back by the metallic sound, the first sound I have made since the accident, but she turns to me and asks where room number four is. She is sorry to bother me at this hour, but the nurses would certainly make her go away if she said she was coming for a visit at dawn. She knows they are very strict about the rules, they would never deviate from the regulations, and visitors are allowed only during the specified hours.

I don't believe it, it seems like a miracle, but words trickle from my mouth and she understands me. And, even more than that, I smile at her and I see clearly that she is smiling back at me. A not very pretty woman, not young, but her eyes are soft and good.

She is observing the floating bed and the instruments with their flickering lights. She puts down her handbag and looks around; I think she wants to sit down. Apparently she is in no hurry to get to room number four, perhaps she is afraid. Then she asks me: *what is your name?*

Gil, I answer without hesitation.

I am Rachel, she answers; she pauses and then she asks why I am not sleeping at this hour. I don't know how to answer: perhaps I should explain that I have no peace of mind and it is only at dawn that no one disturbs me, perhaps I should say something about the accident, but I don't know how to describe it so it's better to ignore it altogether. Finally I reply that I have trouble sleeping. She smiles again and says she normally sleeps at this hour but today she got up early to visit her cousin, who is hospitalized in room number four, severely ill, she wishes to visit him when no one is around. But now, her face turns sad and she removes a lock of hair from her face, she is scared to go into the room and see him ailing, perhaps on his deathbed.

I look at her and wonder whether she really came to my room by accident. A soft woman, wearing a delicate grey sweater, childlike curls surrounding her head; one could tell that only love for her cousin could have made her enter the corridors of the hospital. She is observing the room with disgust, and clearly she is eager to get out. She stares at the bed, which in this early morning light reveals light stains and dust, then she peeks at the small sink in the corner of the room, and finally she looks at the machine, whose orange lights keep blinking endlessly. Finally she turns her gaze to me and asks if I know where room number four is.

I want her to stay but force of habit makes me answer that in the corridor she needs to turn left; I am surprised that I know this. A feeble smile appears on her lips, she turns to the door, but then accidentally her leg hits a chair, she almost trips, her handbag falls down, and various books and papers spill out and spread around.

I am nervous, I would like to get up but my body is planted in the bed and I can't move. Rachel is extremely embarrassed, all her belongings are visible, wrinkled papers, napkins from a restaurant, a red lipstick without the cover, exposed and chipped, a small bandage that rolls on the floor and disappears under one of the beds, a couple of books, some closed, some open, their pages torn and wrinkled. She is beside herself, so ashamed, looking around in despair and not knowing where to start picking up her things. But then I see that the tall night-shift nurse is standing at the door, her face full of restrained anger. In a quiet voice, too quiet, she asks Rachel who she is and what she is doing at the hospital at this time, why is she bothering patients who need to rest, why is her stuff spread all over the room?

Please collect your stuff and get out of here immediately, if you don't want the hospital security guards to come and throw you out at once.

Rachel is blushing, she mutters something about a cousin she came to visit, she kneels on the floor and collects her things. She stretches a thin hand first to the papers, then to the books, and finally she tosses a couple of pens into her handbag. The tall nurse is standing still, watching her with her blue eyes narrowed as if a wild animal is in the room, and someone has to be called to capture it and remove it, like a soldier on guard, willing to protect the patients from any form of danger. Finally Rachel gets up, manages to pick up the heavy handbag, turns and looks at me with her soft eyes and smiles, as if we share a secret. Then she turns to the door and walks away. I try to follow the sound of her footsteps, to see if she stopped at room number four, but the tall nurse begins to complain out loud about people bothering the patients at unacceptable hours, and so Rachel disappears and I don't know if she ever found her cousin.

Finally the nurse with the blue eyes is gone. I can't stand her smile, it's worse than the face of the somber, sad nurse who, in her purple clothes, looks so exhausted that she can't spare a smile or a kind word. The tall nurse, on the other hand, keeps smiling, willing to engage in small talk at any time.

Morning. My mother is here again. Today she seems to have recuperated a little; her face is not as pale as it was; now there is some tranquility in it, an acceptance of an unavoidable fate. She looks at me with a certain distance. In her hand she holds a fresh tissue, which she uses to clean my face. The tissue scratches me and is unpleasant, I feel as if she is writing on my face with chalk. But when I try to move my head the pain penetrating from my neck is so sharp that it reaches my throat, so I give up and let her paint my face, a diagonal line on one side of the lips, the same line at the other side of the mouth, and then she connects the two lines with a strange sketch on the chin, but she fails to make a nice triangle so she keeps redrawing the lower line. Finally she looks at me with satisfaction: apparently she has managed to create an attractive geometrical shape.

She sits next to me, her face displays her devotion, and she is trying to make conversation. All her stories are about a person she calls *your wife*, and someone who is probably my daughter.

In a low voice, intended to emphasize the seriousness of her words, she tells me about how they have been suffering since the accident. I have already heard about the *accident* but I still don't understand exactly what happened to me. I know two cars crashed into each other and dropped together into an abyss, but I am not sure where I was during the accident. My mother is not trying to explain, she repeats the description of their suffering over and over again: they cried all day at home, at night they couldn't sleep, they felt everything was lost, it was so hard for them to see their loved one suffering that they preferred not to come. She spices her description with words like *misery, disaster, accident, despair, homelessness, agony,* they are all part of her story, and I can't help observing that they are all aimed at a certain end; in devious ways she is trying to convince me of something. I am not sure of what, I don't understand how the vivid descriptions of their agony are going to convince me of anything, but it is clear she is trying to get somewhere. Her eyes are half-closed: sometimes she reminds me of an actor on stage facing a small and sleepy audience, so in order to create excitement he stops acting and begins to believe in the tragedy he impersonates.

She speaks for several minutes and then she is exhausted. She gets up and looks at me closely, makes an expression resembling a smile and says again: *Gil, my Gil, would you like to eat something?* I refuse. All the food she makes is tasteless. My mother insists on bringing something every time she comes, but I detest the food she draws out of her handbag: mashed banana, a salty pie that burns my lips, a mushy, almost liquid cake, a yogurt she mixes so hard it loses its texture. I stop myself from spitting the food out. Once, it came out of my mouth involuntarily. She watched me as if I were a sick child, immediately took a plastic spoon and tucked it into my mouth, like someone trying to feed a stubborn baby.

After a couple of hours she leaves, and I fall asleep. Sometimes sleeping is so pleasant; I return to the cave and it is so good. The sound of splashing water is so gentle that I need to listen attentively in order to hear it. But when I manage to hear this rare xylophone my spirit is lifted, I am full of hope—maybe I will manage to escape from this white room with the bed floating in the air. I am alert, trying to hear this rare elusive tune, when a pat on my face wakes me up.

Again it is the curly-haired woman, the one who sits on my bed and touches my body in a familiar manner. She is smiling, her eyes are contemplative, and only her mouth is moving as she says softly: *Gil, did I wake you up?* Another sound of a drop touching the cave's floor, I try to absorb one more consolation, but she doesn't let go, she hugs me with fingers stained red at their ends. She touches me with determination: her thin fingers pat my cheeks, run through my neck and reach my chest, to the left side, then to the right, and back. From there they turn in a circular movement to my stomach. All her movements are peaceful and moderate, she acts as though she is fulfilling orders, carrying out a plan enforced upon her, and I think that there is a striking similarity between her and the nurse with the somber face; she, too, washes me with straight movements, according to a predetermined rhythm, beginning with my head and continuing to every part of my body. But the curly-haired woman is also smiling as she touches me, she sits on the bed and mutters soft words, calling me *Gili*, and sometime she turns to me and says

my love

My heart aches as I hear these words. Her hand on my body gives me such pleasure but her words are stabbing. As she murmurs love words I am waiting for her to get off the bed, to pretend she would like to stay but she has to leave, and to walk on her high heels to the door, careful not to show any haste. I don't know why but I am deeply relieved to see her disappear. Yet her hand touching my body gives me much pleasure, I would be glad to let her fondle me everywhere, she could even remove the painful bandages, I would move my head from side to side in spite of the cast made of sharp wheels in order to see the thin hand running over my body. But as she turns to me and demands that I admit I know her, insisting that I remember things I find utterly strange, I can't wait for her to leave. The palms of my hands open, my breath is not heavy anymore, my head is falling slightly backwards, and I close my eyes. She feels my resignation, tightens her mouth—a slight insult passes like a cloud across her eyes, but then she comes to her senses, puts her head next to mine; her lips touch my lips, they are soft and gentle, a bit wet, they flutter on my mouth and it is impossible to tell if they kissed me or not.

Tonight a new man came. Though he is also wearing a blue suit deadening sunlight, his entire appearance is different from that of the doctor. He is a short, very sturdy. I see his muscular arms beneath his suit. He approaches me, carrying needles and straps for blood tests. I am anxious, he seems preoccupied with his work and doesn't look at me at all. His movements are all aimed at completing the job quickly and joining his friends who are sitting in the corridor. He bends his head and looks at the needles, his thick hair falls on his forehead, concealing his eyes, and then I see his huge square hands, the palm much bigger than the thick fingers, seizing the needles carefully so as not to twist them. He is holding my arm, sticking a long needle into it; I am surprised since he causes no pain at all. His great hands with the gross fingers use the needle as if it was a magic tool, which even a boy could use easily. Surprise makes me moan, and then he lifts his head, looks at me with his small, oblique eyes, and says: *sorry, did I hurt you?*

Strange, his words have a unique melody: he articulates them with a different, unfamiliar tune, some syllables are too long, others are short and distorted. For a moment I think he is talking in a foreign language, but he turns to me and apologizes, he is doing his best not to cause any suffering and he wishes he could treat me while I was asleep. With an effort I speak and say that he is not causing me pain, if I weren't looking at my arm I wouldn't have noticed the needle at all. I find it hard to articulate the words but I wish he would stay with me for a while. He smiles, his face reveals suffering but still it is also illuminated, he puts away the needles, bends down towards me and says plainly: *hello, I am Sergei.*

His entire expression is altered. At first he was eager to conclude his task and walk away, now he stays to look at me, examining me and trying to evaluate my medical condition. With the same weird tune he asks if my bandages were changed, and would I like him to care for me. I don't answer, but Sergei knows I want to place my body in his hands. He brings his head towards me, examining every wound with concentration, looking at every scratch. Now I realize that my body is full of bruises, some not even bandaged, a strange mosaic of white bandages, red and blue stains, my head is apparently hairless, and my neck is frightfully painful. I watch Sergei. I don't know why I encouraged him to nurse me, he could have taken the blood test and walked away. I feel there is something bestial about him, the heavy arms, the palms that look as though they were made for hunting, the thick hair, the slit-like eyes, but his touch is as gentle as one could imagine. Sergei removes the bandages from my head, indifferent to the foul odors of blood and cavities, examining the gaping wound with concentration, determining whether it should be cleansed and covered again. He brings a bottle with a transparent liquid, wets a cotton pad, and stretches it towards my head.

Horrible fear startles me. My body is shaken by the dread of pain, before he touched me I could feel my skin torn away. But Sergei is smiling at me; he takes the cotton pad and cleanses the wound. His movements are direct, unhesitating, he causes no pain, the cool liquid is pleasant, the wound is gaping and the scab pulls away easily. The open skin is placed in his well-trained hands. I surrender to the touch of the cotton pad on the wound, all the while enjoying the lack of torment. Once the wound is clean he brings a new bandage, stops for a moment to plan in which direction it should be applied and, after considering various possibilities, tapes the white cloth to my head, leaving me tense and exited. Then he turns to me and asks in his unique tune: n*ice? Should I go on?*

He spends a long time replacing blood-stained cloths with white bandages, clean and pleasant. Only once was my skin pulled by the bandage, and my cry made him shiver. He almost dropped the medications. He apologized immediately, he didn't see that the body and the soft material grasped each other so strongly. His movements became even more cautious, and every time he added medication to my body. When he was done replacing all the bandages, he lifted his head and looked at me; several drops of sweat accumulated on his forehead, he smiled and said that his work was done; now I have to go to sleep, there are only a couple of hours until dawn. Before he leaves the room I feel that I am sinking into something resembling a cloud. I lie on soft, pleasant bedding and I can hear once again the sweet sound of water drops splashing on the floor of the cave.

Morning. As I open my eyes I see my mother sitting next to me, absorbed in reading. She doesn't see I am awake, so I can examine her face without attempting to please her. She is a little bent, wears dark, heavy glasses, and her face has an almost childish expression. She wears a purple dress with a print of tiny flowers. Next to her she puts her big handbag, full of food she has brought for me; her hair is in wild but clearly she did try to straighten it out. I look at her quietly, and now I realize I can turn my head more easily, the teeth of the cast supporting my neck are not so sharp anymore. After a couple of minutes I clear my throat and she removes her gaze from the book, trying to read one last line, then looks at me and smiles. She gets up and stands beside me.

Her questions are terribly bothersome. She feels that if she doesn't ask me how I slept, if I have eaten, if I feel somewhat better, I won't know she is worried. She is wrong. I can see very well that even when she is not next to me she feels the odor of the hospital, and she wakes up thinking she is beside my bed. Her entire existence is concern and worry. But lately I see a submissive look in her eyes, revealing some acceptance, a look one often finds among very poor people: an expression of weakness, as if they are well aware that they can never overcome the obstacles darkening and constraining their lives. She is trying to appease me, afraid that I will see her despair. Immediately she offers some sweets, a drink she made at home, a pack of salty cookies she feels are soft enough for me to eat. I am not hungry but I comply with her wishes and eat a little bit so I won't have to see the disappointment on her face.

After I take a bite from the cookies she begins telling me about relatives who keep calling her to ask how I am. She spells out the names; I don't know who they are. She tries to explain, *do you remember Uncle Joseph, the brother of your dad who died several years ago? He was the eldest brother, dad was the youngest. He was very attached to you, ever since dad died he was like a father to you, you asked for his advice in professional matters, he was married to Bracha, a tall, graceless woman who calls very often to tell us about her children, she also likes you a lot, when you were a kid she used to bake a cake on every birthday, she loves to cook, when she invited you for dinner you always went because of the gorgeous food.*

My mom looks at me helplessly, like an industrious ant she is trying to collect any piece of information from my past, to drag it into this white room and load it on a pack of stories she assembled earlier; but she feels that all these tales, half false, tend to lose their vitality as they materialize into a successive description of my life. Like a torn necklace, its beautiful beads spread everywhere, my mom collects them all and arranges them in the exact order, but to her utter despair the string is broken and cannot be repaired.

Her failure is reflected in her petrified eyes: she is afraid I will disappear in a space in which all strings are detached. Without words she knows that I feel sorry for her, that I am touched when I see how much she cares about me, but the umbilical cord was cut off with a blunt blade, melted away in the burning heat of the accident. She is searching my eyes endlessly for a piece of memory, a hint of the past—but I can't recall anything. In order to avoid her desperate eyes I try to think of something that preceded the accident. I close my eyes, attempting to ignore the white room—which lately I have noticed is not so clean and has some stains—eager to remember something. All I can hear is a terrible noise, a huge grinding of metals clashing, irons bending in heat and twisting, creating a sound that could be described as ringing: like a giant bell that should have made a deep, pleasant sound, but instead is being swung forcefully from side to side, and the only thing that is heard is a deafening metallic clank, a terrible rasping voice, shocking and eerie, and whoever hears it is begging to leave the bell untouched, since the sound it makes is crippling.

I wake up from sleep and my mother isn't here anymore. I feel something pleasant fluttering on my arm, climbing on it; perhaps an insect. The touch is so gentle that I am sure it isn't harmful. I open my eyes. Now I turn my head easily, and I see the beautiful girl again. Her hair is tied behind her head, her innocent eyes watch me, the straight eyebrows are stretched outward, she is smiling, and her finger runs along my arm. I think patting me makes her happy. The palm of her hand is rounded with dimples, she moves it down my arm and then to my hand, careful not to touch the bandages and the needle stuck in there. She caresses every finger, with concentration, as if she can't remove her hand without fondling every part of mine.

I can't take my eyes off her. Her beauty makes me examine her over and over again, tracing every small detail: the soft skin looks like lustrous velvet filled with tiny pebbles, the brown eyes, full of sunlight, watch me with a childish puzzlement, looking at every part of my wounded body, the straight brush strokes above her eyes get close to each other, she is absorbed, then she stretches her childish hand back and lets her hair down. A wave of red bursts out instantly, its ends are touching me, and a couple of hairs creep into her rounded mouth. With a childish hand she removes the strands gently. I watch her, amazed, wondering how this angel has come to my bedside to rescue me from my agony. She is smiling at me and then she says:

daddy, do you remember me?

No, I don't remember her. I think I never saw this angel outside the walls of the white room. But I am so eager for her to stay that I hear the words coming out of my mouth, *yes, sweetie, of course I remember you, you are my daughter, my love.* I am afraid she will ask me her name, demanding proof for the memory, but she is so pleased that she asks for nothing. She is smiling, looking secretive, as though she has managed to reveal a hidden plot, a secret plan that only the two of us share. Then she suddenly halts, taking her hand away from my arm and standing motionless, focused on an invisible spot on the ceiling. I am breathless, I don't understand what happened—perhaps she realizes that I don't remember her? But then she slowly lowers her head, on her lips there is a hint of a different smile, more like feminine suggestiveness than a childish giggle; her eyes are enigmatic, perhaps seductive, and through her rounded lips she filters: *can I tell mommy?*

The girl runs and disappears behind the door, I hear excited cries outside, a loud voice and a deep sigh, someone is coughing, and the familiar voice of the man emitting orderly, disciplined words. I am anxious, maybe I shouldn't have said that I know her, but I wanted her to stay so much that I lied naturally. Then the thin woman with the curly black hair bursts into the room. She walks gracefully on her high heels, her face more colorful than usual, strange stains on her cheeks make her look doll-like; again I think she is about to take out a lollipop from her purse, or gummy bears, and chew them with gusto. But she approaches me rapidly, the smile on her face resembling a twitch, something that may precede crying. She bends her head towards me and kisses my lips.

If it weren't for the twitch I would gladly succumb to her kisses; but they reflect an effort in her that makes me turn my head away. Something about her is too devoted, as if she is attempting to complete an imposed task. Though I look sideways, trying to turn my head, she sits on the bed easily. I am embarrassed but she is determined to keep kissing me, and then, to my surprise, she puts her feet on the bed and lies on top of me. Her light warm body covers me; she puts her arms around me; her head sinks on my neck. I feel my thin, almost transparent, skin between my ear and my shoulder, a childish remnant at the sides of the head, and upon it I sense long wet eyelashes touching me like a feather, and afterwards several drops rolling slowly toward the white bed sheet.

My heart is pounding. If I could move I would get up and walk away; or perhaps embrace her. She is lying on top of me as if the voices emerging from the corridor don't exist. After a couple of minutes she lifts her head, runs a thin finger on my face, smiles—I am not sure if she is younger or older than the girl—and says in a metallic voice:

Gili, have you woken up?

Disgust fills me. I feel I can't take the weight of this woman anymore. For the first time my hands obey me, I manage to move them though they are carved in stone: my muscles are fully strained. In spite of the pleasant, soft warmth of her body I push her away, careful that she shouldn't fall from the bed, but I am determined to stop her from sinking into the sides of my neck. She suddenly seems too plump. I realize that in spite of her childishness there is something rounded about her, her stomach is even slightly protruding. I can't take her body leaning on me. She is surprised I can move my hands but she doesn't understand I am trying to push her away. On the contrary, she is smiling at me, her eyes are bright, the floating brown islands seem almost glamorous, circling within the green balls. She sits at the edge of the bed, her legs crossed, and again her hands run along my body; I am not sure whether the stains at the ends of her fingers are blotted with my blood. Kindly, almost laughing, she turns to me and asks: *would you like anything, Gili?*

A huge rock begins to roll down from the summit of a mountain. At first a terrible creak is heard, a scream emerging from a desolate valley in which no man has ever set foot. The dark gray cliff shakes slightly, jolts, and then slowly it is torn from the mountain on which it lay for many years. An immense stone, full of bumps and bulges, with antique stones and skeletons of ancient reptiles embedded in it, splits and begins to move downwards. At first it rolls slowly in an undefined direction; there is no knowing if it will fall into the abyss or halt. It appears as though the motion has stopped and it will now find a new abode for thousands of years. But the momentum increases gradually, advancing and freeing itself, another roll makes a squeak, another turn grinds various plants, and the mass is galloping forward, stampeding quickly towards the abyss. Here, it reaches a cliff, now it is detached forcefully, falling down, it is so huge and heavy that is seems that when it strikes the ancient valley it will keep on rolling until it stops; but as it touches the ground everything erupts, a sound of explosion fills the valley and its echoes are heard over and over again from the surrounding mountains. A huge cloud of dust and stones ascends. And only after the air, saturated with soil particles, begins to sink, can one see that all that is left are endless small grey pieces, a broken mosaic whose parts are forever lost, and again the valley is filled with primeval silence.

The bed I am floating in begins to move. I don't know what has happened, but I can see very well that I am sailing on it to a new place. Endless lights above go by. I ride in strange corridors. A man with a sallow face is pushing me, he seems extremely alert, as if it was very urgent to drive me to an unknown place. I see that the woman with the curly hair and my beautiful daughter are running next to the bed, holding hands, watching me in horror. I don't know what is wrong, they stampede after me as if there was an obscure competition between them and the man pushing the bed. The curly-haired woman begins to cry, the tears cover her makeup; she seems a bit strange, but I see she is alarmed. And as she manages to get close to me I can hear, in between her heavy breathing, that she keeps saying to herself:

what have I done, what have I done?

I don't understand, I am trying to figure out what is going on, why everyone is running, and what did the curly-haired woman do, but the swift movement of the bed is uncomfortable, jolting me. Once again I feel pain in the neck, a wound opens and blood begins to drip on the floor. The beautiful child is horrified as she sees the red trail left by the galloping bed, she also begins to weep, the full, pretty lines of her eyebrows are distorted, the pebbles on her face are washed in a river of tears that can't be held back. We reach a new place, harshly lit, the light is so bright that it is impossible to see anything. We are about to go through a door, I look at my beautiful daughter and hear her scream, frightening the people standing in the corridor, in her childish voice she is crying and yelling:

daddy, daddy, don't go.

I go through a wide door; it is shut right behind me. Now I am in another room, a new woman dressed in purple approaches me, and to my utter surprise places a mask on my face. I find her humorous spirit surprising, she is making me wear a costume, perhaps that of a clown, since she places the mask on my nose and mouth. But I feel she doesn't find my costume amusing, she looks extremely serious. Then a couple of people enter the room, they watch me and whisper. I want to know what they are talking about but I can't understand a single word. I think they are only articulating syllables, perhaps it is a foreign language. The woman with the purple suit sticks a huge needle in my arm. I am terrified as I see the thin tube that is about to be inserted into my body, but she is very dexterous and I feel nothing at all.

Now that I am wearing the mask I realize there is a breeze of fresh air beneath it, it reminds me of the wind in the cave; I have almost forgotten the constant pleasant hum there, infiltrating into the twisted rocks and sneaking out with a gentle whisper. The wind hits my nostrils with pure air, as if it was brought especially for me from snowy mountains. I feel my body light as a feather, almost drifting, there is no need for the floating bed anymore for I am so light that I find it hard to stay on the white sheets, hard not to part from them and rise towards the ceiling.

The light hum becomes somewhat louder, like wind blowing through a valley surrounded by mountains, striking the bushes on the slope, bending stalks of yellow flowers blossoming in between the rocks, and shaking the pine trees growing diagonally on the hillside. But suddenly the wind changes its direction; before it blew the dry pine needles down the hillside, now the thin, brown threads are flying upwards to the mountain, rising up without falling. I watch amazed, wondering how come the leaves are not falling down, and not only that but the cones are flying with them, tossed upwards above the treetops, striking the sharp heads of the pine trees without falling down.

In a panic I try to unravel this wind, but then I feel it is absorbing. It grasps me, my body is stretched, my legs are still entrenched in the bed but my head begins to spin, it hits a strong whirlpool of air and can't escape it. I am scared. I look at the strong lights in the ceiling. I detest their blue tone but still I try to use it to figure out where is the window through which this draft is coming, a gust that almost tears me from my place.

The blue lights of the room seem more agreeable now, purplish, shimmering in a majestic splendor. A strange, unfamiliar sense takes hold of me. Something folds into itself, consumed, converges inward. I think my hair is falling out, my two legs feel as though they are becoming one and my hands merge into my body. Fear fills me, I think I will disappear in a moment, the blowing wind will take me with it and I will fly upward like the cones. But I am left on the bed, my head is still lying on the pillow, though I can't move it to see if my body has been left unchanged.

Perhaps I am hallucinating. I don't know, I think the room is filled with a pink light and an aura is visible in the distance, there is no knowing where the light is emanating from. Now I see tiny lights glittering at both sides of the room, maybe they are miniature candles, sparks emerging from different places and moving slightly in the wind. I don't understand where these two flickering rows come from, it is as if a swarm of fireflies was caught in the room. Now they stand one after the other, flickering their tiny wings and buzzing, ready to fly out. The room looks somewhat golden; in spite of the dark night, sunrays penetrate. I wonder how come sunshine is glowing at midnight, day and night existing side by side without blending, the sunlight doesn't remove the darkness.

I strain my eyes and see two strange ruptures, elongated circles surrounded by black decorations. I don't know what they are—

perhaps transparent leaves holding raindrops, but their color is weird, slightly golden, and the black protuberances around them are moving from side to side. These strange leaves keep shrinking, I don't know why. Now they look like a new moon, a stomach protruding between two stalks, yet these bodies are also becoming exhausted, and in a minute they will disappear. I am terrified, the golden light coming from behind the leaves fades away and instead a new light emerges, dim, looking like it is emanating from itself. Now the two moons have vanished. A thin crust covers me, pure silk, whose threads are slightly torn, here and there red ends are hanging, they look full and rounded but their ends are unstitched, splitting into endless fine and tender hairs.

I am back in the cave; once again I hear the sound of water splashing on the floor, but this time I think it is falling from a high place, like a waterfall flowing into a stormy river. I am not sure why but the voice is not as pleasant as it used to be. I am eager to smell the plants growing on the sides of the cave, but in vain. The cave is strange to me, I feel a gust of wind but I don't know where it is coming from. Astonished, I sense that I am falling, my body is dropping downward slowly but without halting, like a mild hover, gliding on a soft, cradle-like cloud, sinking constantly. Though I feel the fall I am not anxious at all: I know nothing can stop this slow descent, and as it advances I stop wondering where I will end up, and I am completely alert, breathless, my eyes are wide open and I look around, I see that I am going down into a deep abyss between gray cliffs. At first the rocks are covered with wild plants, sharp and jagged leaves, curved stalks, flowers so fleshy that I find it hard to watch them, protruding red, thick tongues. From among the trees, so high that their tops can't be seen, I hear menacing growls like the voices of wild animals watching their prey and howling at the poor, exhausted animal, waiting yet another moment before they insert their sharp teeth into the still-living flesh. I try to follow the howl but all I can see is a gigantic alligator tail, bony and bold, disappearing between the trees. As I am sinking the plants gradually disappear, only stag-like thorns can be seen on the hillside once in a while. Finally bare rocks surround me, cracked and split, looking as though they were ruptured by an eternal sun, ancient crags, and now I see they are immersed in lucid water; the purple light is vanishing, fading and consuming itself, a spot absorbing any light beam. Darkness prevails around me, but to my surprise I see that this darkness is illuminating, strange but true, in an obscure sky overshadowing the rocks I can see better than ever, and then I see

ABOUT THE AUTHOR

Emanuela Barasch-Rubinstein is a writer and a scholar in the Humanities. Her parents fled their homes in Eastern Europe and immigrated at to Israel, and Emanuela was born in Jerusalem. Her father was the noted art historian Moshe Barasch. Emauela studied in the faculty of the Humanities at the Hebrew University of Jerusalem. Her PhD is in Comparative Religion and Literature. She was part of the Comparative Religions graduate program at Tel Aviv University; now she is part of the Nevzlin Center for Jewish Peoplehood Studies at the Interdisciplinary Center (IDC) in Herzlya. She is currently living in Tel Aviv.

Emanuela began her literary writing following the death of her father. Her book: "Five Selves" will be published by Holland House Books in 2015. It is a collection of five novellas, addressing the issue of Israeli identity, explicitly and implicitly: generation gap in Israeli, coping with death and mourning, capitalistic values of Israeli society and, finally, the dying self.